THE BEST SMALL FICTIONS

2015

THE BEST
SMALL FICTIONS
2015

Guest Editor
ROBERT OLEN BUTLER

Series Editor
TARA L. MASIH

FOR QUEEN'S FERRY PRESS

2015 Consulting Editors
Kathy Fish
Christopher Merkner
Robert Shapard
Claudia Smith

2015 Roving Editors
Michelle Elvy
Clare MacQueen

General Assistance
Heather L. Nelson

Cover design by Brian Mihok

Interior design by Steven Seighman

First edition October 2015

ISBN 978-1-938466-62-5

Printed in the United States of America

CONTENTS

FOREWORD

In 1952, an American named Robert Oberfirst began to publish an annual series he eventually titled *Anthology of Best Short-Short Stories*. The collections appeared until 1960, when the series ended. Eight volumes were collected, including both reprints and commissioned stories from writers unknown to us today to those we recognize as some of our greatest U.S. literary icons: William Faulkner, Jack Kerouac, and Ray Bradbury, for example. He also included iconic writers from abroad, such as V. S. Pritchett.

The demise of this series celebrating the very short forms, as opposed to the similar series that began in 1915 that recognized the longer short story and still continues today (*The Best American Short Stories*), reflected the general loss of interest in periodicals where the very brief stories appeared for decades, and an academic world that considered these brief stories formulaic, at best.

Today, in part because of the groundbreaking *Sudden* and *Flash* anthologies edited by Robert Shapard and James Thomas, journals proliferate that promote the short short, more commonly known now as Flash Fiction, and academic programs are beginning to accept the teaching of this form, along with the evolving short prose hybrids. Therefore, the time is right to bring back the Oberfirst series with a new title, a new look, new forms, and a new commitment to find the "Best Small Fictions" published worldwide.

Because this is our first year and the press and I believe in transparency, I want to explain our process, which we've developed in order to be as objective as possible. Queen's Ferry Press publishes this series, but has no involvement in the selection process. Official nominations come directly from editors and publishers, and finalists are selected by me and my team of consulting editors, who rotate each year. We also consider unofficial nominations made by outside editors who point us toward stories, but mainly from two roving editors, who read for us and remain anonymous until winners are announced. Their role is very important. They find fictions that might get overlooked or are published in journals that might not nominate.

The finalist list is narrowed down (we intended to have 100 this year, but the quality was so high, we selected 105), then our esteemed guest editor selects 55 "winners." Queen's Ferry and I believe all our finalists are winners, but recognize that some fictions may still achieve more than others. These winning fictions, from diverse cultures all over the world (we received nominations from 11 countries, including translations), are judged to be the best of what we receive in traditional flash form and in its subgenres: micro, Twitter fiction, iStories, fictional prose poetry and fictional haibun, and anything in between. We also select speculative, horror, and graphic small fictions. The final judging is blind.

Why do we feel compelled to declare that anything is a Best Of? It provides a rubric that's necessary for evolution and improvement. To have examples our best practitioners select gives students of the genre something to shoot for and experiment with, instructors something to teach, and writers a small but official pat on the back for the countless hours they've spent writing into what they often feel is a dark void. I got many thank-yous from writers expressing how important this was for their psyche, but none said it better than Anthony Martin, whose small fiction was nominated by *Cheap Pop*: "Not only am I honored, I'm extra jazzed that small markets and presses are taking the time to promote the little pieces of people's hearts floating around out there. It means a lot to someone like me, as I'm sure it does to the other nominees."

Acknowledgments: Thanks first and foremost to Queen's Ferry Press for making this possible. It's been delightful working with publisher Erin McKnight and Kevin Wehmueller. They provided the perfect home. Thanks also to Brian Mihok for the wonderful retro cover design and to Steven Seighman for the classy interior design. Next, we would not have as much interest in this new series without the name of Robert Olen Butler. QFP joins me in thanking him for accepting our small press project, and for guiding us not only to the Best Of from the finalist list, but in other matters that set the professional tone for the series. We can't thank him enough. To my wonderful consulting editors: Kathy Fish, Christopher Merkner, Robert Shapard, and Claudia Smith. They took time out from busy teaching schedules to provide stellar opinions. Thanks also to roving editors Michelle Elvy and Clare MacQueen. No longer anonymous, they've been promoted to Assistant Editors. Their help this first year was invaluable; they reached out to some important international editors and found many gems that became finalists. (Clare was particularly instrumental in bringing the international fictional haibun community aboard, and we are pleased to represent, perhaps for the first time in a Best Of volume, this new hybrid form of haibun.) Heather L. Nelson assisted with general outreach.

Thanks to the dedicated editors and publishers who took the time to select, nominate, and mail in their authors' fictions. To celebrate your journals and presses—for the hard work you do in soliciting, editing, publishing, and promoting, often with little payback—credit lines are prominent. In addition, we spotlight a journal or press that's represented by the most winners or finalists. It's additional work to nominate, we know, but Martin's statement proves it is important and appreciated.

While readers may not "like" or approve of every small fiction selected, we have no wish to censor language or ideas and are confident readers will see value in each of these original fictions and the high level of craft that they set for others to reach.

Finally, this series is dedicated to Robert Oberfirst, whose vision continues in *The Best Small Fictions 2015*. We hope he would approve.

—*Tara L. Masih*

A SMALL INTRODUCTION

Most everyone interested in writing and reading works of fiction of a very short length has struggled for years to name these things: flash fiction and microfiction, nanofiction and sudden fiction, short short stories and liminal stories and even Yasunari Kawabata's elegant "palm-of-the-hand stories." Tara Masih and her editorial staff shrewdly have named the works in this much-needed annual anthology "small fictions." The shrewdness was for them to identify these works as fictions. Not stories. The 105 finalists they then sent me were fascinating in their diversity. Some of the fictions you will read here are full-fledged stories, including the smallest one, at 27 words. (I explain what I understand to constitute story in my essay, "A Short Short Theory," which appears in Masih's estimable *Rose Metal Press Field Guide to Writing Flash Fiction*.) But empowered by their smallness, to be fiction all they need to do is lie. About large fictions, which, by their length, must have plenty of story in them, Carlos Fuentes once said, "A novel is a pack of lies hounding the truth." A small fiction is a lone wolf of a lie, sometimes hounding the truth across a field but oftentimes simply sitting on a hilltop to raise its face to the moon and howl of love or loss, pain or fear, hard-earned wisdom or benighted ignorance. We listen to small fictions like nightsounds from afar. They enter us briefly, in sweetness or sassiness, in hilarity or aching sadness, but they leave us imprinted with freshly experienced truth. Truth possible to know only through the clarifying lies of fiction. Take your time with these, please. A few at a sitting. Read them slowly. They are small but brimming with our shared human experience.

—*Robert Olen Butler*

BY HEART

Dee Cohen

From *DimeStories: California, New Mexico, and Beyond!*
(DimeStories International, 2014)

Now it's winter, almost night, and the young girl is sitting at the kitchen table writing and rewriting her spelling list while her mother slams open and shut cabinet doors.

Words can be so tricky: sometimes *right* is R-I-G-H-T and other times it's not. It's hard to keep them straight. She feels her mother's irritation growing. It's taking too long for the girl to catch on. She should have these words memorized by now. And here's new trouble: *slight* keeps turning into *sight* and she's erased these words so many times that the paper has holes and small tight accordion creases. Soon her mother will look over the girl's shoulder and see the damage done. Out of the corner of her eye, the girl tracks the small degrees of escalation—the anger tightening her mother's back, twisting her mouth.

Sometimes the rage can sit for days in the bristles of the hairbrush or the tines of a fork. Sometimes it pools on the bottom of the tub or is soaked into the sour smell of a washcloth. Mostly it resides in her mother's forefinger: the point, the jab, the blood-red polish, the way it drums on the Formica counter. You never know where it will turn up.

But it is always somewhere and it is the girl's job—her occupation—to pay close attention. Because if she doesn't, she might get her hair pulled, or four long fingernail gashes down her arm that burn like they're on fire. Bright with fire:

B-R-I-G-H-T

Strange how years later, the smell of that past fury will float up from a chiffon nightgown in a thrift store or from an open jar of Vaseline: all the oily products meant to slick the girl down, keep her flat. Or how the stylish objects from the '60s—pointy fenders and pointy eyeglasses, pointy shoes and even pointy breasts—still look like weapons to her. The girl feels fear rise up from her stomach, move into her throat.

F-R-I-G-H-T

Out the window, the streetlights come on, small haloes of warmth. *Light* with a silent *gh*. She doesn't know that these evenings will stalk her throughout life. That her mother's frustration will dig its fingernails into her arm and hiss at her through clenched teeth for years.

She looks down at the paper at the last word—the hardest word to spell: *Height*. An inside-out kind of word. The great distance from which she'll always watch herself, hovering overhead while the young girl learns these lessons again and again by heart.

•

DEE COHEN is a poet, prose writer, and photographer living in Albuquerque, New Mexico. Her work has been published in various journals, including *Spillway, Kimera, Perihelion, RipRip, Poetry Super Highway, Mal Pais Review, Adobe Walls, Mas Tequila Review, Anthology of Orange County Poets,* and others. Her book of poems, *Lime Avenue Evening,* was published by the Laguna Poets, and she was a Featured Poet for Duke City Fix.

A NOTICE FROM THE OFFICE OF RECLAMATION

J. Duncan Wiley

From *Pleiades*, Vol. 34, No. 1, Winter 2014

The Division of Reclamation, Mining, and Safety would like to remind everyone that abandoned mines are dangerous. Last year, twenty-two people across the country died while exploring such sites. Victims suffocated in oxygen-depleted atmospheres, fell from broken ladders, and drowned in near-freezing pools of water. They were crushed by cave-ins, poisoned by carbon dioxide, and fell through holes that opened beneath their weight. They encountered rattlesnakes and mountain lions; they triggered stores of unstable explosives; and they fell—oh, how they fell—three hundred twenty, one hundred sixty, nine hundred feet to their deaths.

We understand the urge. We are human. We too have come across those dark, sighing cavities in the earth's crust, a few gray timbers or rusting rails lying scattered around their mouths. You see such a place, and you know that people have gone that way before. You know the passage was safe once. Then you start wondering: What's it like inside, just beyond the reach of sunlight? Did those others leave anything behind? What if there's a seam of gold or silver, just waiting for you to discover it? We know this urge, know how strong and primal and erotically charged it is. But before you rush off to penetrate the mysteries crowding your imagination, we say this to you: Resist.

The earth does not give her secrets up lightly. Rocks grind their granite teeth over geologic eons, holding their grudges close. You cannot win against them. Your little flame of curiosity, infinitesimal by comparison, will gutter before it illuminates even the shallowest depths of that darkness. You will fall.

Or you will not fall. Any number of calamities could claim you.

But most likely, you will be swallowed by a vertical shaft. We know this because the vast majority of the bodies we recover are bashed and broken, having plunged hundreds of feet through jagged tunnels. There is no telling how many we haven't found. Perhaps some have never stopped falling. Perhaps there are one or more bottomless shafts full of people tumbling forever down, down, down. We don't know. We heed our own advice and do not go exploring. Anything might be possible in the farthest, forgotten reaches of these mines.

We are inclined to believe that every shaft ends, and every fall down a shaft ends badly.

Imagine, for a moment, open space. Imagine yourself unanchored and weightless, pitching head over heels through nothingness. Imagine also air that is like chilled copper, thin and brittle and sharp around the edges. Feel how it pinches your lungs. You could be breathing copper foil for all the pain in your chest. Everywhere there is a formless sound. You cannot tell if it is the air itself, chiming like millions of low-voiced copper bells, or if you are hearing the slow groans of tectonic plates, amplified here beneath the surface. You wish you had brought a warmer jacket. Both your flashlight and your sense of up and down are gone. Darkness is absolute. All you know for certain is that somewhere a bed of solid rock awaits. You rush toward it, or it rushes toward you, or you rush toward each other like blind lovers.

This is what we think it must be like to fall three hundred twenty, five hundred eighty, nine hundred feet down a mine shaft. The only mystery is when and from what direction the end will arrive. We warn you: There is nothing for you here. All you will find is an oubliette for your bones.

Still, you do not listen. We know that even now you are entering open adits; you are cutting the locks on our safety gates and steel doors. Before you take one foolish step more, we say this to you: Stay away. Some things should remain buried. Leave the ghosts and the echoes and the earth's seeping wounds to us. They are dangerous. They are ours.

•

J. DUNCAN WILEY's prose has also appeared in *Cream City Review*, the *South Dakota Review*, and *Bayou Magazine*. He lives with his family in Nebraska.

HAPPIEST BLACK WHITE MAN ALIVE

Dan Gilmore

From *Serving House Journal*, Issue 10, Fall 2014

"Little Harlem," they call it behind the Santa Fe station middle of LA's black ghetto.

But when you walk inside that building half the size of a football field with a ten-foot-high ceiling and a dance floor moon-dented by years of spiked heels and shined by see-yourself-in Florsheims when you walk inside carrying your drums and cymbals and you make your way through that thick cigarette smoke trapped by that low ceiling you're not anywhere near the train station. And if you're me, you're inside a scared white boy's skin, an 18-year-old last-minute fill-in drummer for Ray Byrd's all-black big band.

And when I walk in and the talking stops and I hear whispers, *Who's the white kid?* I trip over my feet and do a little hop and try to walk with that black-swagger thing but I feel like a performing seal.

First set goes okay. We play every *My-man's-done-left-me* song, every *All-I-want-is-my-baby-back-so-my-heart-can-sing* song, and I'm laying down the money beat that sharp backbeat on two and four and I'm feeling good.

Then at break Byrd says, *We gonna turn it up a bit.* And I say, *You mean faster, louder, longer?* And Byrd says, *Yeah. One-eighty for the full set* and I say . . . *Fine.* But I know when I play that fast for that long my body locks up can't move my feet can't feel my hands can't breathe and I'll sit there a statue of myself entombed in my own flesh turned to stone.

So Byrd counts off—one-two, one-two, ugh ugh. It's fast all right. Trombone guy solos five minutes then a little trumpet player dude then Byrd honks his tenor sax for twenty minutes—on his knees, on his back, humping the air while cigarette smoke snakes through the room through a thousand perfumes thick bourbons scotches all mixed with face sweat breast sweat crotch sweat fishnet thigh sweat and the dancing doesn't stop. It'll never stop as long as I can keep hitting that backbeat but I'm tightening up and I'm scared I'm gonna miss it and the whole place will freeze in disgust because the white drummer kid just blew the fuse on a thousand black souls because he hit on one and three instead of two and four. I'm counting and praying I can last for twenty more minutes so I can stop jerking off atop this ticking metronome of white logic.

Just then Byrd gives me that sulfur eye that vaporizes me because it's his *Time-to-take-your-first-solo* eye. So I start real soft like brushes on white bread. People start drifting toward the bandstand. Someone snickers. More join in. Not knowing what to do and afraid to keep doing the same thing, I kick the bass drum, BOOM, switch to sticks and start this double-time riff off the left hand. It sounds good. Where it comes from I don't know. My right hand tumbles from little tom to big tom while my bass keeps that BOOM BOOM ba-ba BOOM thing going and my high-hat is crisp as Byrd's big wink. Heads start nodding to my beat bodies too. Then the sound of my drums bounces off all the walls and we're all back in some jungle part of ourselves circling a fire hands flying cinders popping. Life, I mean LIFE is flowing from a place where nothing is good or bad, just IS and there's almost too much happiness and I give the eye back to Byrd who is wrinkled-eyed smiling. And I hit a final lick, pause a beat then BOOM kick the band back in. Trumpets squeal bones moan saxes join in with a rocking riff and the whole band rides that same riff. Trumpets go higher and higher until it's impossible to go higher then damn if the little dude trumpet player goes even higher up a whole octave and holds that high note while the band riffs louder and louder and if you're there inside my electric skin you're thinking the trumpet player's head is going to explode then Sweet Jesus, he goes higher yet and you stop thinking and everyone is clapping and grooving and it doesn't surprise me when I look down I see my hands have turned black arms too all of me has turned black clear through and there's that feeling when old pains and pasts old fears and loss don't exist and nothing is left 'cept ALL that's good and pure and me smiling so big it hurts, 'cause I never felt this full before, 'cause I AM the happiest black white man alive.

•

DAN GILMORE has published a novel, *A Howl for Mayflower*, and three collections of poetry and monologues, *Season Tickets, Love Takes a Bow,* and *Panning for Gold*. He has won the Raymond Carver Fiction Contest, the Martindale Fiction Award, and multiple Sandscript Awards for Short Stories. His poems have appeared in *Atlanta Review, San Diego Reader, Aethlon, Blue Collar Review, The Carolina Review, Sandscript,* and *Loft and Range*.

MARRIAGE

Anna Lea Jancewicz

From *matchbook* lit mag, August 2014

When she was waiting tables, she used to marry the ketch-up bottles. That's what they called it, *marrying*. Taking two bottles that are less than full, making them one. But the joke was on her.

She figured the punchline while the veil was perched on her head like a ghost sparrow. While she was still waiting on him, off on a beer run with the best man, sure he had at least thirty minutes to burn before he had to hit the altar. But it was too late by then, the dress like a Portuguese man-o-war and the fifty-six chicken dinners were bought and paid for.

It's not like there's this third bottle. There's the bottle with the least left to give, upended. And then that bottle is empty, the other gets it all.

•

Anna Lea Jancewicz lives in Norfolk, Virginia, where she home-schools her children and haunts the public libraries. An associate editor at *Night Train*, her writing has appeared or is forthcoming in *Atticus Review*, *Hobart*, *Phantom Drift*, and *Wyvern Lit*. She is working on her first novel.

A DREAM WITH THE WIND IN IT

Kelly Cherry

From *GARGOYLE* #61, Summer 2014

After their deaths, her parents still visited her. Well, mostly it was her mother who came. Even when her father tagged along, he tended to stay off by himself, in a corner. As he'd always done. Her mother would come up to the foot of the bed and call her name until she woke up. Though the room was dark, her dream was suffused with reflected light, a dreamy moonlight, and Michelle could see her mother, who was wearing a work shirt and underpants, clearly. She used to walk around the house like that when Michelle was a teenager. The shirt was one of Michelle's father's shirts, with the sleeves pushed up.

Each time, Michelle asked her mother what she wanted, but her mother never answered. And yet her mother seemed so sad that Michelle was sure that she must want something, and it drove her a little crazy not to be able to figure out what it was, because it must be something she expected Michelle to give her. An apology, perhaps. Or forgiveness.

Or love.

But Michelle had given her so much love when she was alive.

But perhaps it had not been enough.

Perhaps it was never enough.

In the morning, lying in bed, Michelle watched the green sleeves of the linden brushing her window. Even with all the traffic noise—the angry rush and howl, the scowl, of it—she could hear the birds' grace notes, trills and frills. And still, in this light, her parents were there, though fainter, like blood spots fading with time.

Pale as a memory from childhood, her mother was leaning toward her, and calling her name, and Michelle heard it like a wind from a place that was always cold, even in early summer.

She lived in Pierre, South Dakota. She worked for a cartage company, invoicing householders arriving in town, departing town.

One night Michelle woke to her name being called, and in the moonlit dark she saw her mother painting the walls of the room white. Paint stuck in her mother's hair like bird droppings and frosted her mother's bare legs, her no-nonsense forearms. The hairs on her mother's arms were like the gleaming branches of a tree after an ice storm. She asked her mother why she was painting in the middle of the night like this. Her mother turned around and seemed about to answer, but all she said was Michelle's name, again, and while it was all right to hear it like that in the dream—which was not quite a dream—it made a sound like a draft of wind, and it chilled Michelle, it really did, even in early summer.

It was the way her mother said it, as if she were deeply lonely in death.

And yet Michelle's father, too, was there. Her father and her mother were together, as they always had been.

Michelle woke, feeling a prairie wind sweep across the deserted terrain of her heart. She thought of her mother and father and how alone each must have been in life. She saw the linden leaves casting a latticework shadow on the white walls of the bedroom, and she heard the birds in concert. She wanted to tell someone she was innocent. It wasn't my fault, she wanted to say, but to whom could she say it, ever? And when she tried to say it, aloud, there in the room by herself, it came out sounding like her own name, like the name Michelle.

One night as she lay in bed, Michelle saw her mother's breasts—wilted, in old age, like flowers past their bloom—try to fall forward, but they were like two flaps of skin with no fat inside. Her mother straightened up again and the breasts somehow folded themselves back upon her mother's sternum, flat as a child's, and her mother's arms became wings folded into her sides, and now her mother was a vulture, huge and impassive, waiting at the foot of the bed.

Then Michelle heard a voice and thought it was her father's, thought the place he was calling from was cold and dark, with a wind reaching out of it like a tempest. Her mother touched Michelle's foot with an outstretched wing, and Michelle felt that the voice and the touch were going to take her away, the wind was going to bear her away. She knew she had to lift her eyelids, even though the force of the gale pushed them shut. Making an enormous effort she opened her eyes, and it became clear to her that the voice she heard was her own, calling to her out of someplace cold and dark inside herself.

Michelle woke, and it was night—or it was morning—and—whether it was night or morning—she was always cold, even when the birds sang, the cardinals like blood spattered on the sky. Once, her mother was running up long columns on the adding machine; once, she was stringing bones on the clothesline in the backyard.

In the moonlight the bones were as white as if they'd been painted. Michelle watched her mother in the yard, the long, shapely legs bare and foreshortened beneath the work shirt.

It was as if her mother were dancing down there in the yard. It was as if her mother were busy with some important work of art.

She wondered how her mother could be so energetic, so enthusiastic about whatever it was she was doing. It took all the energy Michelle had, it seemed to her, merely to sleep each night and dream, a dream with wind in it, a dream that could carry her away.

•

Kelly Cherry has won numerous awards for her writing and recently served as Poet Laureate of Virginia. She has published 23 books (including *A Kelly Cherry Reader*), 9 chapbooks, and 2 translations of classical drama. Her 24th book, *Twelve Women in a Country Called America: Stories*, was published by Press 53, and her latest chapbook, *Physics for Poets,* was published by Unicorn Press.

FOR THE WHEELS TO NULLIFY

Brent Rydin

From *WhiskeyPaper*, August 2014

I lost my shoes in Greensburg, Kansas. The earth was rutted out in ways nobody could see, and I'd expected something solid there beneath the mud but there was just more mud, up to the knees. Everyone else had just gone around it, but I trudged through. My then newly ex-girlfriend took a picture of a street number on the curb and a front path leading into weeds and dirt and sky, and someone commented online a year or so later, "That's where my parents' house used to be." I threw my socks in a garbage can and rolled up the cuffs of my jeans.

We drove down these long stretches of road, through cows and sky and Oklahoma and Texas and Kansas, at 100 mph while everyone else was driving the opposite direction. We were in the van, all staring at a red splotch on a satellite screen in the dashboard and I wondered if tornadoes spun the other way around in Australia. We went to the university where one of the guys worked and he talked about weather balloons and we drove down a street named for the Flaming Lips and I ate chicken-fried steak and we watched as a barn turned into an airborne swirl of planks and hay in a minute flat.

She and I lay as far as we could from each other, on top of polyester motel bedcovers pulled tight, me facing the wall and her facing my back. I could feel her hand stretching out, just barely. "I think I'll take the couch, actually," I said.

We headed toward wherever we were going, and I sat in the passenger seat as Dr. Weather Balloon drove. It was something like two in the morning, and the rest of the van slept. He said his wife was divorcing him. "Shit, man," I said. "I'm sorry." I'd known the guy for three days. "Thunder Road" came on the radio and he turned it up just loud enough to make out the words.

Chasing tornadoes isn't scary. That's not bravado, saying that—tornado chasers, we were just the assholes who watched from a safe distance, and we drove fast and circled the danger and skirted anything real.

I stood under a green sky and crouched and protected my head and let hail like walnuts pelt at my back and arms and neck. "Get back in the van," they shouted, and I pretended not to hear them through the blankets of wind.

•

BRENT RYDIN is the founding editor of *Wyvern Lit*, and has work published or forthcoming in *Pithead Chapel*, *The Island Review*, *Cartridge Lit*, *WhiskeyPaper*, *Chicago Literati*, *CHEAP POP*, *Noble / Gas Qtrly*, *Synaesthesia Magazine*, and elsewhere. He can be found in most corners of the literary Internet, along with a few coffee shops scattered throughout New England.

NOT ABOUT LIZ

Catherine Moore

From *Tahoma Literary Review*, Vol. 1, Issue 1, August 2014

There is a fence between one moment and the next: the black of this bay sparkle on a breakwater, the dappled gray in stacked rock encircling a field. That field, and that fence, it took careful climbing to breach, as I remember from age eleven. And it's odd—smelling farm grass and watching hooves shuffle, along the seaside.

I'm saving up for a Wild Mustang, Liz always said; *they're unconquered.* My childhood friend ever hopeful, ever bright. Liz the delighted and doted on, not overlooked like Jana Ray Jones and her bed-tanned mother. Too busy with her big hair rollers for school start times, at each stoplight came another minute-long blast of Aqua Net. Her spray swaths the back-seat: first Jana Ray, then Julie Ray, next Jarrett Ray. I stayed second-hand safe in the front seat, wondering why there wasn't a new middle name for each disposable child. Maybe it was the vapors. The busy social life. Maybe she didn't care.

Not like Liz's parents—always home, always watching. Her dad looming at the sliding glass door. Her mother the kohl eyes behind the upstairs curtains. A cloistered place without all the holiness clung in air. And darkest in Liz's bedroom, no bigger than a stall, where she wanted me to come, sit, and see her horse dolls. *I have to show you my new Appaloosa! My daddy just brought it home.* Those foot-high plastic molded creatures lined the shelf along her headboard as if on guard. In that room with a riding crop and whip always wound up on the back of her bedroom door, *someday I'm going to ride for real*, but that leather looked worn. And the creepy horses: I didn't like how she laid back reaching overhead for them, braying *neigh, neigh*. Or when she invited me to lie with her to watch in frightened fascination as she held an invisible rein, lifted her pelvis, moved in a make-pretend gallop, *neigh, neigh*. I'd have a hovering sense to bolt. The way the smell of something wrong lingers and warns you away.

The way I'm back to smelling hooves on sod. Watching rocks skip along the bay. And the rocks fall way down, down into an old meadow on top of all the pretty little horses, her favorite Appaloosa, the blacks and bays, dapple and grays, *neigh, neigh.*

Those are mine, shouted over the pink cotton panty stretched between us, crotch twisted thin, at my slumber party. *No, no, I have a pair just like them.* I let it go, knowing we weren't both Sagittarius. I let it all go, the gray of the braying and French-kissing, and the black in the time she asked, *Does your daddy kiss you goodnight? How many times?*

•

CATHERINE MOORE won the 2014 Gearhart Poetry Prize. Her work has appeared in *Grey Sparrow, Ars Medica journal, Southeast Review*, and *Pankhearst Press*; *Story*, her poetry chapbook, is available from Finishing Line Press. Catherine earned an MFA from the University of Tampa, Florida, and volunteers as a literacy tutor.

INLAND SEA

Stuart Dybek

From *Ecstatic Cahoots: Fifty Short Stories*
(Farrar, Straus and Giroux, 2014)

Horizon, a clothesline strung between crabapples. The forgotten dress, that far away, bleached invisible by a succession of summer days until a thunderstorm drenches it blue again, as it is now, and despite the distance, the foam of raindrops at its hem sparkles just before the wind lifts it into a wave that breaks against the man framed in a farmhouse doorway.

BRISKET

Stuart Dybek

From *Ecstatic Cahoots: Fifty Short Stories*
(Farrar, Straus and Giroux, 2014)

Their pale, plump skins scorched almost to bursting, the Thuringers invited a plaster of brown mustard.

The stacked pastrami was decked out in zooty 1950s colors: blushing pink meat in a carapace of black pepper.

There was corned beef awaiting horseradish, kosher franks and kraut, dangling salamis, *tukus*, house hickory-smoked turkey, trout, sablefish, and two kinds of knishes—thin kasha and golden squares of potato—slaw, paprika-dusted potato salad, fried onions and schmaltz, green tomatoes, kaiser rolls, baguettes, pumpernickel. I'd been walking around all day in the cold and it all looked good. But finally, when my turn in line arrived, I decided to invest my last few dollars in the garlic-kissed brisket on rye.

"Young man, I'm going to make you a very nice sandwich," murmured the old, bald server, wearing a stained white apron.

He said it conspiratorially, his lips barely moving, drawing me toward him in order to hear, as if it were something he'd rather the owners of the establishment not get wind of. A secret between the two of us, not for the ears of the others behind me in line.

He glanced up into my eyes and held them as if he'd taken a personal interest in me, which was more than I could say for the secretaries and interviewers in the personnel offices where I'd spent the last six weeks filling out applications for jobs while my money ran out and I moved from friend to friend, crashing from apartment to apartment, sleeping on sofas and floors as if I'd never grow up if I stayed poor. His face, crosshatched in lines, was set in the comically tragic expression he'd practiced until it had become his permanent physiognomy. He must have been making sandwiches for a long time, must have seen a lot of hungry faces staring back at him from the other side of the glass partition.

Maybe he'd learned to read faces at a glance and could read in mine that a desperation I'd never felt before was setting in. That I needed a helping hand. That I'd caught enough of a glimpse of what it meant to be down, homeless, jobless, walking the streets hungry to last a lifetime.

Or maybe to get through the day he allowed himself now and then to take a liking to the face of a perfect stranger. A face that perhaps reminded him of himself when he was young, or of someone in his past, the way that, riding the subway and watching all the people with jobs filing on, I'd sometimes see a woman who would remind me of an old girl-friend in another city, a city I should have stayed in, a girl-friend I should have stayed with. That same girlfriend who once told me, "You've got a working-class face."

Maybe he thought so, too.

"See?" he said, surgically trimming off the fat with the tip of his carving knife, and then scraping the trimmings across the cutting-board counter, leaving a trail of grease. That's when I noticed the numbers tattooed on his wrist. I'd seen the faded marks of the death camps on the wrists of tailors in that neighborhood before. Those tattooed numbers still shocked me into a sense of dislocation. The brutal reality of history crowded out the mundane present. I wondered what he thought when he looked at his wrist every day. What horrible memories did he overcome each morning? When I saw those numbers I felt ashamed. Here I was spending my last few bucks—big deal! I would survive.

"How about some nice scraps for your dog?" he asked, gesturing with his knife to the pile of trimmings that he'd been accumulating from mine and other sandwiches. Attached to the fat were hearty-looking ribbons of brisket. There was at least another meal there.

"Sure," I said.

"Okay," he said, still with that confidential tone as if something preferential were going on between us.

Working in a practiced methodical sequence, he wrapped the trimmings in waxed paper and the waxed paper in a sheet of brown butcher paper which he expertly folded into a neat, tight, easily concealed packet before taping it and handing it toward me. "Only two dollars."

"Two dollars?"

"For your dog," he said.

I thought he'd been offering to give them away and suddenly I felt like a total fool. All at once it struck me that whatever had made me naïve enough to think the scraps might be free was the same impulse that had landed me in my current situation: out of work, living from friend to friend, missing a woman in another city, a woman who'd already given up on me.

"I don't have a dog," I told him.

"You just said you had one."

"I used to have one."

"You forgot you don't have a dog anymore?" He couldn't get over that someone could make such a mistake.

"I had a dog but he died. I still say yes out of force of habit."

"I'm sorry to hear about your dog."

"Thanks," I said. "He was a schnauzer named Yappy.

Happy Yappy I used to call him. He sure would have liked those scraps."

"Maybe you have a cat?"

"No cat," I said.

"You sure now?"

"Positive."

"Want a garlicky pickle with that?"

"How much?" I asked. I'd learned my lesson.

"Comes with the sandwich."

•

STUART DYBEK is the author of five books of fiction—*Ecstatic Cahoots, Paper Lantern, I Sailed with Magellan, The Coast of Chicago,* and *Childhood and Other Neighborhoods*—as well as two collections of poetry, *Brass Knuckles* and *Streets in Their Own Ink.* Dybek is the recipient of many prizes and awards, including the PEN/Malamud Award, an Arts and Letters Award from the American Academy of Arts and Letters, a Whiting Writers' Award, four O. Henry Awards, a MacArthur Fellowship, and a Guggenheim Fellowship. He is distinguished writer-in-residence at Northwestern University.

EAT BEETROOT

Jane Swan

From *Flash Frontier: An Adventure in Flash Fiction*, April 2014

Mariana ate sliced beetroot straight from the can, as if it were a sacrament. The disc, not quite the colour of blood, dripped as she put it onto her tongue; she held it there for a moment, chewed and swallowed.

Greg came in to get his jacket. Mariana's back was straight, her dishevelled hair tumbling down. Wispy—like baby's hair, Greg thought. He turned and left for work.

She did not hear his good-bye, entranced by the starlings flying into the macrocarpa hedge, dry grass dangling from their beaks. They landed on the branches and disappeared into the tangle of foliage.

She ate another piece. The beetroot's strong, earthy flavour was masked, but only just, by the vinegar.

"A hamburger's only a hamburger if it's got beetroot in it," she said. "I've eaten a whole can. What does that make me?"

Mariana's feet were cold. She had no slippers on, only the dressing gown she'd scrambled into to go to the bathroom. In the toilet bowl was her blood. An icy slab had slammed down on her.

Ice numbed; ice froze. Ice kept things the way they were.

Would she begin to feel something? Anything? Her emotions had flown away like the starlings. She wouldn't try and collect them yet. The thing to do was to settle. Land on a branch where it was safe.

Replenish the blood. Eat beetroot.

•

JANE SWAN lives in a seaside village north of Dunedin on the South Island of New Zealand. She is happiest when writing and making, or in the company of family and creative friends. Jane has had fiction published online, in print, and broadcast on New Zealand's National Radio; has been Highly Commended in the *Heartland* competition and shortlisted in the *Sunday Star Times* Short Story Competition; and has also published nonfiction.

590

Stephen Orloske

From *Nanoism*, 590

Twitter Fiction

No one is watching how I weep into the earth, thought Abel as his brother's cudgel fell again, that now there is neither one God nor many.

•

This sentence by Stephen Orloske won *Nanoism*'s 5-year Anniversary contest. While Stephen writes, his other eye is on the moose stalking in the backyard.

THE THIRD TIME MY FATHER TRIED TO KILL ME

James Claffey

From *Mojave River Review*, Winter 2014

I lay on the bed for three days and waited for the swelling to subside. My left eye wouldn't open and the world through my right one was a sunburst, even through the closed drapes and the wet towel that covered my bruised face. We'd been at the neighbor's house, for a "session." Fiddle. Bodhrán. Tin Whistle. Bushmills. Guinness Extra Stout. They were Northerners. From Derry. Provos, my father said. Sympathizers. *Sotto voce.* They sang and clapped and stomped shod feet on hardwood floor, the smell of man sweat and bomb-making thick as perfume.

•

When it came to the end, and they played "The Green Fields of France," the players roared, "Did they beat the drum slowly, did they play the pipes lowly? / Did the rifles fire o'er you as they lowered you down? / Did the bugles sound 'The Last Post' in chorus? / Did the pipes play the 'Flowers of the Forest'?" They raised glasses, and the main singer cried, "I . . . I . . . IRA, fuck the Queen and the UDA," as everyone drained their drinks. I said something about how the Queen didn't seem so bad, and my father bristled.

•

Fuchsia bushes, a monkey-puzzle tree, and my mother's prize roses the only witnesses. My head hit the railings again and again. Blood fizzed and ran down my face, a warm stream, and he said, "Never defend that bitch again. Never. Do you hear me?" The earth spun as he dragged me to the front door. My mother screamed when she saw the state of me. "Leave him alone. Bloody Royalist," he said. She helped me to the bedroom and brought ice and whiskey for the pain.

·

The second time he tried to kill me we were paddling in the waves at Brittas Bay. I was dog-paddling in the water, looking for sea creatures in the clear ocean. Mam was smoking a fag in the shelter of the windbreak—the striped one with wooden stakes—and she couldn't see us from her vantage point. "Would you swim properly," he said, pulling at my arms and trying to show me how to move them over my head, the way Johnny Weissmuller did in the Tarzan films. I sank, my lungs full of water, his foot on my back, holding me under. Maybe when my arms stopped twitching he got nervous, because next thing I knew, I was on the sand, lying on my back, and him pushing on my belly until the saltwater spumed skyward and I turned blue to white and gulped air.

·

The first time my father tried to kill me, I was swaddled between both my parents and couldn't stop crying. The curtains were pulled shut, the room black as my mother's insides. He kept muttering, "Aw, for Jesus' sake, can't you quiet that babby?" She tried. Soother. Gripe water. Rocking. The lot. I cried on into the small hours. She must have fallen asleep from exhaustion, and he placed his hand over my mouth and nose and pressed down. Only the 5 a.m. milk delivery cart and its rattling bottles saved me. She woke to the tinkle of glass on glass, and he pulled his hand away like a bad school-boy trying to steal a few sweets from a jar of Bulls-Eyes.

•

JAMES CLAFFEY hails from County Westmeath, Ireland, and lives on an avocado ranch in Carpinteria, California. He is a fiction editor at *Literary Orphans*, teaches high school for a living, and is the author of the short fiction collection *Blood a Cold Blue*. His work appears in the W. W. Norton anthology *Flash Fiction International*.

MAMA SAYS

Casandra Lopez

From *DimeStories: California, New Mexico, and Beyond!*
(DimeStories International, 2014)

Mama says, never let a man hit you. Never let one bruise you purple or crack your bones like a wishbone. Never let him snap you in half, until you're cryin' in the street for help. Mama says, there will be none of that for you. I'll teach you how to poison a man before I let that happen to you.

When you are older, mama says, I will tell you the rest of this story. For now all you need to know is this. Once there was a woman, who was a little girl, just like you, but she dreams every day about escaping her daddy's house. It's a dark house, not like ours. A house where all the kids run to hide when their daddy comes home. That's all I will say about that, except as this girl gets older, she tells herself that there's got to be better places. And when this girl is not quite a woman, she thinks she sees love in a man who looks nothin' like her daddy. He's wiry and white, hair the color of dried-out straw. Daddy don't like it when he comes around. She has to sneak out windows and back doors, but that don't matter when you think you are in love, but really you are in love with the idea of love and most of all with escaping.

One day the doctor tells her she's gonna have a baby. And even though she don't know what she's gonna do with a baby, she lets it grow big within her and waits and waits. But she doesn't let her daddy kick her out of his house. She leaves before he can say anything to her. And she is a little too proud of that fact, that her man says she can live with him. Her man is good at making all kinds of sweet-sounding promises that she lets herself believe in even when he grabs her arm a little too rough, so that she can't help but tear up, even when he yells at her not to.

Mama says, back then this woman was young and dumb. Back then, she don't know much. She says, that girl-woman don't exist anymore. She's a buried bone, someone's half-wish, a dried-out seed that a hot gust of wind up and blew away. Mama says, even a young girl like that can learn to say enough is enough. Even if you don't say it outright because you're being kicked down, and don't remember how to speak words that make sense. But you still have enough sense to call for help. And after that, that woman don't call that man her man anymore, so when her daughter is born she don't have to call that man daddy. Mama says, I tell you these stories so you know, never let a man hit you.

•

CASANDRA LOPEZ is a Chicana, Cahuilla, Luiseño, and Tongva writer raised in Southern California who currently lives in Seattle. She has an MFA from the University of New Mexico and has been selected for residencies with the Santa Fe Art Institute as well as the School of Advanced Research where she was the Indigenous Writer-in-Residence for 2013. She is a CantoMundo Fellow and a founding editor of *As/Us: A Space for Women of the World*.

WINTER

Kathryn Savage

From *SAND: Berlin's English Literary Journal*, Issue 10, Fall 2014

He was married, and so was she. This hadn't dissuaded them but set the precedent. Kept it equal. Yet more than that, it made them happy. He had eyes the color of the lake. He watched her when he fucked her. She felt like the little island in the large lake, small inside green water. He was a large man. His arms were trees, his body the sky. Her stomach was shadowed, dark and light and his.

Gone now both, husband and man. The lake is iced over, children skating across it. She is the kindergarten teacher. But when she was in love with either man, especially the man who wasn't hers, she'd lift a child up and smell his hair. Like wet sand, the little boys smelled like wet sand, and she'd say into his hair, *There is mystery.* The little boy would shriek. There was a swelling up inside her at that moment, grotesque and huge, and she would free it, biting the tips of the child's corn-silk hair, pressing her nose to his head.

•

KATHRYN SAVAGE holds a BA from The New School and an MFA from Bennington College. She has received fellowships and support from the Bread Loaf Writers' Conference, the Ucross Foundation, and the Vermont Studio Center. "Winter" was inspired by James Salter's "Dusk."

SCARLET FEVER

Stefanie Freele

From *The Chattahoochee Review*, Fall/Winter 2014

Simultaneously, she is seven years old dressed in a white sweaty nightie and forty-seven years old covered in sweaty snow pants, a down jacket, and her husband's blue long johns, the ones with shredded ankles. This can happen when an illness bridges across a lifetime; both sicknesses occur on different planes, different paths, interjecting, interloping, running side by side like two rabid foxes eyeing each other, running, salivating.

The scratchy couch, made of a wool/acrylic blend, reaches through the sheets to sandpaper her young skin. With a fever, 100 percent cotton sheets are best, cool and soothing. Later in life, she will realize she is allergic to polyester, which is but one of many reasons for this misery. She has been moved downstairs next to the kitchen, perhaps so her mother does not have to climb the steps to tend to her. Not that she's tending anyway, the girl is soaked, moaning and being told to hush. She is seven. Hush.

Thinking of seven—when she is forty-seven and has pneumonia—of this itchy nubby couch spattered with peanut butter and crumbs, the high window with the white pressing light and the hope she placed on the light in that window, *fix me.*

Little girls do not normally visualize themselves as adults, but here she is dripping, picturing water spilling from under the house, blue warm water, knowing her older self is also inside her chest, inside her head, they are together in a fever. She tells this to her mom, *Another me is here, but I'm forty-seven.* Maybe she tells it to her mom, she's not sure she has said this out loud and she's not sure anyone is there, as she can't see over the back of the couch. To sit up would take concentration, effort. There is no cup of water and she needs a cup of water. *Bring me water, please,* she says to the white window.

Although her lungs know she has pneumonia, her mind doesn't yet. The heating pad at her back, the down jacket on her top, and her body stuffed into a flannel sleeping bag—all this and shivering should tell her *you have pneumonia.* An idea of picking up her son from school is running around in her head like a sloppy Ferris wheel that has fallen off its track, from her chin to her forehead, *pick up your son pick up your son.* Also inside her mind: a little girl in bed, she reaches out and it is herself, bringing water, changing the unbearable sheets on the couch, lifting the hot little girl, holding sips. You can trust me, she says. They say it to each other. How can anyone get up and drive?

As if the fence has come down and the water is running out of the yard, her bladder is about to do the same; she can feel how it will roll down her legs, soaking the couch, her hellish nest, but there is no better, *help I need to go.* No one is answering and where is her mother. Water running out of the house into the yard. Feet on the carpet, so rough, so awful on skin, why isn't anything soft, ever? There is nowhere to go when nothing is soft. Dizzy and a small hand on the back of the wool couch and a hand on a wood wall, at least that isn't scratchy, if only she could sleep on a wall. If only a person could sleep standing up or tilt the house. Freezing in the bathroom, it is cold cold cold and if she could only have a blanket and she doesn't think she can get back to the malevolent couch where she can at least be warm. *Mom!*

Please, she calls her husband, *you have to get our son from school, I can't.* There is a weighty sense of guilt, a guilt as large as the playground; how difficult can it be to drive and retrieve your son, your own child? No water next to her. A girl at seven reaches for the glass and fills it over and over, but still the glass is empty and there is no one to ask for more.

Her father presents to her a fox, made of polyester/acrylic, and she wants to hold it, hug it, but it is another offering her skin can't bear. *I'm forty-seven. Cotton.*

Her father stays twenty feet away, across the room by the fireplace.

Did you pick him up from school?

The fireplace without a fire is unfriendly next to her father with his trench coat and his impeccable tie, asking in a faraway voice, *What are you talking about, sweetie?*

Her mother tosses a green washcloth into his hands, a toss of I'm-done, the same washcloth the girl has been turning over and over on her forehead. *She's been rambling, making stuff up all day.*

Barely can she see white over white as she whispers, *Thank you, Daddy,* reaching for the fox while her mother tromps out of the room pouting, *Of all the things I've given her, you buy a cheap airport stuffed animal and she loves that.*

Her husband says, *Get over it,* and sticks a cold hand under the down jacket, laughs. He is her rabies-infested, untrustworthy fox, grinning with enjoyment from shocking a warm body with his chill. She is too weak to hate him, too tired to explain. Water, she hears water flowing out of the house, down the front steps, but none in her mouth. He fills her cup, brings home their son who kisses her forehead and says, *You're hot, get better, Mama, hurry up, I know a new card trick, one with disappearing aces.*

The woman brings the feverish girl closer, to keep each other warm, pressing foreheads together, breathing shallowly while their bodies go about ordering the disorder. This way they can rebuild together. Reinforce the dam while eyelids are burning.

•

STEFANIE FREELE is the author of two short story collections, *Feeding Strays* (Lost Horse Press) which was short-listed for the John Gardner Fiction Award, and *Surrounded by Water* (Press 53). Stefanie's published and forthcoming work can be found in *Witness, Glimmer Train, Mid-American Review, Wigleaf, Western Humanities Review, Sou'wester, Chattahoochee Review, The Florida Review, Quarterly West,* and *American Literary Review.*

LITHOPEDION

Randall Brown

From *Metazen*, March 2014

She delivered her baby twenty years too late, his body turned to stone to protect her from infection. Three days after the operation, she swaddled her son, sat in the taxicab on her way to her apartment in Old City, a few blocks from Independence Hall and the Liberty Bell. The driver kept saying what a good baby she had—so quiet and content. He asked her for the name and she said she still hadn't decided. He threw out some: Marcus, Bruce, Julius. She smiled, said she'd consider them.

Four days later, she met Chas in Washington Square. Chas waited on the bench, tinier than she remembered, a stick figure, bone. His eyes were closed, and she sat next to him, didn't wake him. Waited.

In a sinkhole on Texas's Edwards Plateau, they'd found such a baby from 1100 B.C. Like tooth plaque, someone described, this process of calcification within a body. Chas stirred, startled awake.

"Oh God. I saw shovels, hundreds of them, turning into stingrays." The first thing they'd said to each other in ten years. Imagine that. He blinked and blinked and blinked. "Can I hold him?"

She handed the baby to him. Chas held their swaddled boy to his chest, as if to burp him. "I thought he'd be heavier," he said. "I never thought—" She watched the squirrels squirrel away the nuts, followed the fall of leaves, tried to give him some feeling of privacy. "How did you know?"

"Something they saw in the cervix. Maybe cancer. Maybe not. But they suggested a hysterectomy. More tests, I wanted. And then they saw him." How still and silent their baby was. Chas now cradled him, rocked him back and forth. "They asked if I remembered stomach pains."

"Oh God, Em. That's what those were?"

She didn't answer. He'd accused her of so many things back then, of seeing and feeling and believing in things that weren't real. She'd seen skeleton babies arising out of the pond's mist. Had felt a leg inside, sometimes kicking. Had brutal stomach cramps, and he'd said all of it had to do with her wanting to make her invisible pain concrete. She had been only able to take so much of that, his logic, science, whatever the hell he'd called it.

She reached and he handed back their baby. Strange how she thought of the baby as theirs. What would he say about such a thing? About what invisible desires lay behind it?

"Thanks for calling me," Chas said. "I'm—grateful. I never thought I'd get to hold . . . You know. Of course you know."

"Are you sorry, Chas?"

"Am I sorry? I didn't know, Em. I was just trying to make sense of everything."

The weight of their baby boy on her lap. One might imagine them as grandparents now. Young ones. One might imagine them as happy.

"What now?" she asked him, meaning, *what will we do with him?*

"What would you do?" he asked her finally. "What do you think we should do?"

•

The house, a carriage house once part of a railroad-family's expansive estate, had always made her think of fairy tale hovels, its foundation sunken like tree roots, the surrounding green like the home of the *Teletubbies*, a show she'd watch day after day in that dark afterward, six miscarriages, missed pregnancies, a final yielding to the Fates, giving up.

She walked through the rooms. Here, in this house, she actually felt tall. A remarkable thing. Here this couple manipulated Rummikub tiles, not talking, so intent, then catching each other's look, cracking up so much they couldn't catch their breaths. Here they roasted marshmallows over their gas fireplace, the repairman asking about the caked-on material blocking the pilot light, both of them shrugging. Who knew? Could be anything?

Here they dreamed of you. Here they planned your room. Here they hid the things they bought, afraid to attach the Beatrix Potter wallpaper to the wall, but unable to stop themselves from filling the closet—a Diaper Genie, an Octopus, a mobile of the planets. Here they watched your form fill each room, tumbling over, building a cabin with Lincoln Logs, pushing a tank engine in circles.

She hadn't felt Chas's hand in hers as they left the house, out the back door, down the hill to the pond. He held the baby now. Here they filled themselves with you, conceived you, precious you, Jasper, for you they waited and waited, how long they waited.

•

RANDALL BROWN is the author of the award-winning flash fiction collection *Mad to Live*. His essay on (very) short fiction appears in *The Rose Metal Press Field Guide to Writing Flash Fiction*, he has a story in W. W. Norton's *Hint Fiction* anthology, and he blogs regularly at FlashFiction.Net. He is the founder and managing editor of Matter Press and its *Journal of Compressed Creative Arts*.

THE THEATRICAL PRODUCTION OF LEWIS CARROLL

William Todd Seabrook

From *The Imagination of Lewis Carroll* (Rose Metal Press, 2014)

Lewis Carroll sat in a reserved seat in the theater with his coat over his shoulders and a black bag at his feet. The program read *Alice's Adventures in Wonderland*, and on the inside cover was a picture of thirteen-year-old Isa Bowman as Alice.

Much too old, Carroll thought, picking up his bag and making his way backstage.

He found Isa Bowman tying ribbons into her blond hair, a blue dress falling just past her knees and white stockings sheathing her legs.

"Are you Alice?" Carroll asked.

"I am," Isa said.

"Nonsense. I know Alice personally. I am Lewis Carroll."

"I'm playing the part of Alice," Isa said.

"Which part? The leg? The shoulder?"

"All the parts."

"This is not how I imagined Alice," Carroll said, looking at Isa. He reached into his bag and pulled out a large paintbrush and a jar of red paint. He slopped the red onto her dress, letting it drip onto her stockings and fleck her arms. "I always saw her in a red dress. I don't know where the devil this blue nonsense came from."

"I am not part of your imagination," Isa said.

"And you are much too old," Carroll said, his mind wandering. "To play Alice, that is." He rummaged through his bag again, leaving red fingerprints all over it. He pulled out a copy of *Sylvie and Bruno* and handed it to her. "Read this. It will take years off your life."

"You did not imagine me," Isa said. "I don't belong to you."

"And I should think you are too tall for Alice," he said, producing a bone saw.

The curtain rose and Isa walked onto the stage, leaving Carroll to hack away at his own long, aged limbs, no longer able to tell the difference between himself and his creations.

•

WILLIAM TODD SEABROOK is the author of four chapbooks; *The Imagination of Lewis Carroll*, in which this story appeared, was the winner of the Rose Metal Press Eighth Annual Short Short Chapbook Contest. He is editor of Cupboard Pamphlet, a fiction chapbook press, and his work has appeared in *The Volta, Tin House, Mid-American Review, PANK, CutBank*, and elsewhere.

HOW TO DISASSEMBLE YOUR FATHER'S GHOST (WINTER)

Jonathan Humphrey

From *Contemporary Haibun Online*, Vol. 10, No. 2, July 2014

> "We suffer each other to have each other for a while"
> –Li-Young Lee

The night your father's ghost appears, take his old pocket-knife from the drawer in the study and have him sit down in the chair. First you must cut the apparitions of his ears. He will ask for you to skip them like stones across the wooden floor. He has always wanted to know this sound. Next, you must sever the opaque tongue from the back of the opaque throat. Cast it into the fire. He will smile, as it tastes like bourbon. Close the knife. Return it to the drawer. His heart will be easily retrieved from the cloud-like chest. It must be fed to the dog. Wake the dog and feed him heartily. Your father's ghost gives you this order without reason. Slowly he will stand and walk to the sliding door by the back porch. Follow him out into the snowy yard. Watch as he stretches his arms. Be prepared to stare until morning. When the wrens wake, they will dart through his body until it is riddled with holes. What remains will lift like fog, burnt off by a trepid sun.

were my father alive
green shoots
pierce snow

•

JONATHAN HUMPHREY's poems have recently appeared in *A Hundred Gourds*, *Contemporary Haibun Online, Haibun Today*, and *Modern Haiku*. With a fondness for whiskey and whippoorwills, he divides his time between Lexington, Kentucky, and the nearby Red River Gorge.

REASONS FOR ELEVATORS

Lindsey Drager

From *The Chattahoochee Review*, Fall/Winter 2014

The hook for the story that has now achieved family legend starts with the motion of elevators. The going up and down to move through the body of the hospital. The blinking of numbers as loads of strangers were shuffled from wing to wing. And then the umbrellas, which serve as the narrative's central motif. But these are just emblems. They were discarded years ago, having outlived the child scheduled to be born that day.

She had to go into labor knowing she would give birth to the dead. When she was told, she wanted it out right away. She said she would not be a coffin, her skin the thin membrane between the here and not; she wanted her body back. Or this is how they tell the story. She has never told me.

I don't blame her. Now familiar with my own vehicle for offspring, such news would turn the being inside me into a fleshy brick. We contain different forms of waste—blood, bowel, brain. Occasionally baby.

The parts of the child that never grew: the nose, the nail. The parts of the child that were never lost: the teeth, the hair.

They say she was never the same. But to confirm this, I would have had to know her before, and I was not yet born. Now, when we gather, we can feel the elephant in the room, its mass occupying all that space between speech, hovering above us like a breathing zeppelin. It's then I catch her looking at us as though we are soiled, like we have committed some trespass just for growing old. I can see in her eyes that we will never be forgiven for getting to live.

So I have to excuse her when she turns to me in an elevator one year on the child's un-birth day and says: tell me about the last time you were a victim.

•

LINDSEY DRAGER is the author of the novel *The Sorrow Proper* (Dzanc, 2015). She is a PhD candidate at the University of Denver, where she edits the *Denver Quarterly*.

WIMBLEDON

Seth Brady Tucker

From *Pleiades*, Vol. 34, No. 2, Summer 2014

It sounds like Nadal and Federer are fucking, very slowly, in the living room, and my coffee is getting cold so I stop with the writing which is really obsessively checking Facebook and Twitter and Goodreads and Gmail and Amazon and Gawker and Flavorpill and all the university job boards, and head the two steps into my tiny living room, and find that my girlfriend of two years is masturbating quietly on the couch, watching Nadal and Federer at Wimbledon. So in a way, you could say they are fucking. And so (let's call my girlfriend) Hilary is slowly swirling herself in slow beats to the grunting volleys and serves and approaches on the television, and when she sees me she is startled a bit, but just turns back to the match and keeps right on going, without a word. I stand there for a moment, wondering if I should join in, but before I can get my mind re-engaged with what I am seeing, and take appropriate action, she pauses and says (let's call me Mike), "Mike, can you give me a minute. Jesus. I just want to finish," and just goes right back to swirling herself slowly to the grunt-pock!-grunt-pock! of the match. I go into my narrow kitchen, put a kettle on, and start grinding some beans (*Ha!*) for another cup of coffee, and can see that she's been into my drugs again, even though we fought about it last night and she had even thrown the remote and busted my lip with it. And no, I didn't hit her, even though she deserves it most of the time, and is getting more and more violent every time she steals *my* drugs, as if that makes any sense. And it's probably the drugs. So, she fights with me because she likes the drugs, and we fight because I am trying to keep her off the drugs, which she then steals and smokes or snorts or mainlines and then fights with me over anyway. But now she is apparently also going to beat off when she does my drugs so we can fight over her beating off when she does my drugs without asking now. I finish grinding the beans, which isn't funny anymore, and pour everything into a French press and then set the timer for a steep time of exactly three and a half minutes because this ensures the perfect cup, in my experience.

I've been trying to get clean, haven't touched the stuff in three weeks, but realize it doesn't matter now, and probably will never matter, so get my kit together and tie off and give what's left of my stash a whirl. The coffee is ready, so I stir it with my spoon and it looks like the cup is eating my spoon, and I realize I don't want it anymore, and I don't want any of this anymore. I stand against the wall in the doorway to my living room and pull myself out of my pants and start jacking it furiously in front of her, ready for the final fight, the final moment for everything between us to come crashing down, but I can't even get hard, and it is just me tugging on my flaccid noodle, Hilary sagged against my pillow on the couch, asleep, and Jimmy Connors saying that Nadal is always going to get to the balls that you think are winners, and that if Federer wants to win this match, he's going to have to play through every point as if it is his very last one.

•

SETH BRADY TUCKER is a poet and fiction writer originally from Lander, Wyoming. His first book, *Mormon Boy,* won the 2011 Elixir Press Editor's Poetry Prize and was a finalist for the 2013 Colorado Book Award; his second book, *We Deserve the Gods We Ask For,* won the Gival Press Poetry Award and was published in 2014. A founder and codirector of the Seaside Writers' Conference (which takes place annually in May), he teaches at the Lighthouse Writers' Workshop in Denver, Colorado, and is an assistant editor at *Tupelo Quarterly.*

APOCRYPHAL

Lisa Marie Basile

From *APOCRYPHAL* (Noctuary Press, 2014)

I keep growing & getting bigger, & my hair is soilblack now, but this is not the story, so we drive straight to the center of the Jornada Del Muerto, and our trunk is open & alight with a dozen white candles. we think it must be what god sees, all this small shimmering. I slip into something but almost nothing, my midriff is showing & I move in the way that reminds you of your mother, o don't we all. when you put your hands on my waist you say *baby is this you?* I'm not sure I'm not sure I'm not sure *I am me.* Am I me? in the desert I am me and not me. I'm halfway across the country by mile and by heart, and there are worms in my mouth. but not my mouth. the big swollen lips I've grown into, a starry artifice. the lips of me, the ones I fake, the me that is a distraction from my own body, someone else's temple & someone else's grave.

•

LISA MARIE BASILE is the author of *APOCRYPHAL* and two chapbooks, *Andalucia* and *war/lock*. She is editor-in-chief of *Luna Luna Magazine* and her work can be read in *PANK*, *Tin House*'s blog, *Coldfront*, *The Nervous Breakdown*, *The Huffington Post*, *Best American Poetry*, and the *Ampersand Review*.

LAST EXIT BEFORE TOLL

James Keegan

From *Prime Number*, Issue 61, October–December 2014

"Excuse me, could you maybe help me out with some money for gas and the toll." She smiled. Young, maybe eighteen. Dressed in a white jacket a little too light for how cold it was outside. A dirty fur collar framed her face, washed out in the fluorescent light. Trailer-park pretty. Damaged blond hair.

He had stopped at the Wawa before the bridge as he usually did to piss and grab a coffee for the last push home to the beach. He'd been saying "sorry" to the girl as he turned, as he took her in, but when he saw her face he'd reached into his wallet and pulled out the lone single snugged up against his saved receipts, smiled lopsidedly, said, "All I got," and handed it to her, already heading for his car.

He slid in behind the wheel and set his cup in the holder and thought of the ATM next to the restroom inside, the $400 in his checking account, the girl's shivery smile.

When he walked back inside he saw her talking to the manager by the sandwich counter. She turned, and though he did not meet her eye he registered her smile and worried there was something in it that suggested she'd expected him to come back. It unsettled his charity and made him march quickly to the men's room as if this was the oversight he'd needed to address. The can was empty and he spent a minute looking at his face in the mirror and feeling foolish, thinking how his momma used to shake her head at him and say, "Charley's big-hearted aunt! Soft touch in a hard world."

This time as he made for his car, he did not look for the girl.

As he passed exit 30 for Whitehall Road, he flipped on the radio to the oldies station he liked. He recognized the tune right off and hummed along as the boy's sweet tenor voice from a life ago sang to a girl named Renée, telling her to walk away, that he wouldn't follow her, that no one could lay blame on her.

An image of his first wife, Marti, came into his mind then, her on a pay phone outside a 7-Eleven on a steamy August night in Newark, Delaware, all manner of bugs bouncing and buzzing on the fluorescent light above her head, as he listened to her telling her mom and dad in Vermont that they had made it okay and the new place was nice and they'd have a phone soon. As he approached the next exit for Sandy Point Park, he saw LAST EXIT BEFORE TOLL beneath the larger road sign. He said out loud, "Well, I'll be a fool then," yanked the wheel and crossed three empty lanes to make the ramp in time.

On the ride back he remembered the story from church of the Good Samaritan and goosed the gas a little, and pictured how he'd ask Renée—she'd somehow become the girl in the song as he got back on 50 West—which car was hers and tell her to pull it up to the pump where he'd fill it and then she could follow him through the bridge toll and he'd cover her, get her home safe. He was pleased as this plan allowed him to know for sure where the money was going.

As he pulled in the opposite drive from the one he'd exited moments ago, he could not see her outside, but it was below freezing so she was likely still inside. She wasn't, though. He went to the ATM and took out $50 and bought a couple of packs of peppermint gum. He craned his neck and looked back toward the racks of chips and pretzels, the coffee station, the freezer cases.

When he got back in the car, he wheeled slowly around the parking lot. He wondered about the dark cab of the semi parked around back.

He left the radio off this time, but as he got back on 50 East, he heard again in his head a single line from the song about Renée.

"You're not to blame."

But he was. He knew he was.

·

JAMES KEEGAN has published work previously in *Poet Lore*, *Southern Poetry Review*, and *The Gettysburg Review*. He is a professional actor, currently working at The American Shakespeare Center's Blackfriars Playhouse in Staunton, Virginia. He is also an associate professor of English and Theater at the University of Delaware–Georgetown.

IT WILL NEVER BE DEEP ENOUGH

Jane Liddle

From *Wigleaf*, April 2014

My party is over. Did you have a good time. It's important to me that you had a good time, and that everyone had a good time. I'm lying. It's important to me that you had a great time and that everyone had a great time and everyone got kissed. That includes me. Especially me. Ha. You're funny.

Don't clean up. Sit with me, Garcia. I need you to sit with me. I need to tell you things. Is that all right with you.

I can hear Sam Cooke smile when he says, "Oh, I like this song," when he sings "Sentimental Reasons" live at Harlem Square.

I can hear Carole King remember a time she had great sex when she sings, "You make me feel so good inside," during "A Natural Woman."

Do you have someone. Do you like her. What does she look like. Does she have long hair. What are her measurements. Why do you cheat on her. Am I getting too personal.

I think you don't really love her. I think she boosts your ego because she's beautiful. You like people to see you with her. You get another boost from cheating on her. The more improbable the affair the better.

That's nothing. One time at three in the morning I called the fire department because my carbon monoxide alarm was going off. I figured it just needed a new battery but I also figured it wouldn't hurt to call the fire department. Since it was so early in the morning all the men on call were young guys so I had my choice. I chose two.

Do you think Ava had fun at the party. Do you think Van had fun. Do you think the food was gross. I failed at the quiche but I know the French toast was perfect.

Do you have hopes. Do you have dreams. Do you have goals. Are they in conflict.

I have a hope that I'll be loved by everyone and a dream that I'll stop caring.

Ava doesn't like me. I think she's intimidated by me because guys dig me and I know it. She doesn't like that I know it so she gets competitive. That's why she came with Van to the party. Van is my ex. I invited him and I invited her but I didn't invite them together. But she came with him. I don't care. She left with him.

Oh, you're funny.

You shirt tag is sticking out. There. Now you're perfect.

Who is the prettiest woman you've ever been with. Is she still pretty. That's a terrible thing to say.

Thirty-six. Is that a lot. How many people have you been with. I thought it would be more. You seem like you had a part of your life where you needed a lot of validation. I did. I had that part of my life.

I'm surprised so many people came to my party. Every person I invited came.

Do you experience tiny devastations.

I can't get through the day without being devastated by little things, like seeing a large tree that's sick or meeting an adorable dog that ignores me.

Did you talk to Van at all. Do you think Ava is in love with him.

I always feel blue after a party. I just want to listen to Gram Parsons and drink sherry. I know sherry isn't a thing to drink but I drink it. I like to curl up in that chair by the ficus. I made that chair out of a pallet. It's really comfortable. Go ahead, sit in it.

Do you like chairs. Do you like reading dystopian novels and drinking Irish coffee while sitting in chairs. I thought so.

Van doesn't own any chairs. Well, he has one but it's also a stool. You can't trust a guy who doesn't have chairs. You can't trust him to be generous about your comfort. If he doesn't have a chair then he can't contemplate. He comes across as contemplative but you know he has a book of questions underneath his bed. You know, that little pocket book called *The Book of Questions*.

You have very nice hands. You have a nice thumb. It's a solid thumb, has got some true heft to it.

My hands are too big for me. They're not man hands but they are out of proportion. I clench my hands into fists when someone takes my picture, but not too tight, because then I'd come across as strict. Sometimes I hold my hands in front of me but then I look like I had a Catholic upbringing and that's not the look I'm going for.

I guess I try to go for a rebellious look. A thoughtful rebellion.

What kind of look do you cultivate. Oh, you nailed it. I especially like your plaid pants.

Why won't you stay. You shouldn't be with her anyway. You don't even like her. Well, you don't even love her.

I want to throw another party. Not a dinner party like this midnight brunch, but a dance party. I want no one to come with anyone else. I want everyone to wear a skirt, even the men, especially the men, and I want to serve candy and play Bee Gees. I want to play "How Deep Is Your Love" over and over. I want there to be dancing.

You'd *have* to dance. No one would rather die than dance. Would you rather die than leave. Good.

I think the most romantic way to be loved is to death. I want someone to love me with so much of their heart that their heart stops. Has anyone ever loved you to death. Do you think someone could. Do you think you could love someone to death. Do you think it's impossible for everyone. Do you think it's impossible for me.

•

JANE LIDDLE was born and raised in Newburgh, New York, and now lives in Brooklyn. Her stories have appeared in *Two Serious Ladies, WhiskeyPaper, Storychord, Vol. 1 Brooklyn, Specter* magazine, and elsewhere. You can find her on her blog, liddlejane.

BEFORE SHE WAS A MEMORY

Emma Bolden

From *The Journal of Compressed Creative Arts*, November 24, 2014

I didn't recognize her without her head. The policeman took me to the morgue. He told me to look. I looked. There was an expanse of steel, smooth and inscrutable as any lake, her body arcing towards her neck. Then the savage intrusion of empty space. It was June. I didn't have a cardigan. And for more than a moment she could've been anyone's daughter. It could've been anyone's yellow tennis skirt, anyone's muddied Keds, anyone's shoulder studded with anyone's moles. They had given me a pill. On her right hand, I saw a circle of silver studded with diamonds. When asked, I said, *Yes of course, a day at the park.* The boy who drove seemed scrubbed to the ears. I was impressed with the precision of his haircut. As an infant, she preferred screams to sleep and I told her that she would regret it. I told her that when she was a teen, I'd keep a list of all the songs that she hated and play them, one by one, to keep her awake. I told her I'd turn up the volume as soon as I didn't see her eyes. They had given me a pill. Were her eyes still in the head they searched the forest for, and if they were open, what would they see? One star had gone missing from the constellation of her ring. I imagine: the clean boy sped with his windows down, letting out all the Aerosmith and air-conditioning. I imagine: she said, *How lovely warm, the sun.* When asked, I said, *The ring was hers.* I said, *I know for sure because it was mine.* I imagine: she was singing and the boy was singing and in the backseat, the air was singing. Each leaf pointed at them and their song. When asked, I said, *Let her keep it.* I said, *I gave it to her so it's hers.* And the afternoon had been so heavy with gold. It occurred to me that I couldn't be sure. It occurred to me that perhaps I'd recognized her not by how she looked but how she looked at me, that perhaps that's how anyone knows anything, not by the looking but by the looking back. It had become very late. If I hoped anything it was that she kept singing. It was that the tree came too fast for her to understand good-bye. I was standing in cold air, which was empty space. When asked, I said, *Yes, I am ready to leave.* I said, *Just like that,* and the policeman said, *Yes. Just like that.* And then we were just standing there. And the silence was blue as a sky.

•

EMMA BOLDEN is the author of two full-length poetry collections: *Maleficae* (GenPop Books) and *medi(t)ations* (Noctuary Press). She is also the author of four poetry chapbooks—*How to Recognize a Lady* (Toadlily Press), *The Mariner's Wife* (Finishing Line Press), *The Sad Epistles* (Dancing Girl Press), and *This Is Our Hollywood* (*The Chapbook*)—and a nonfiction chapbook, *Geography V* (Winged City Press). Her work has been featured on Poetry Daily and chosen for inclusion in *Best American Poetry 2015;* she also won the 2014 Barthelme Prize for Short Prose from *Gulf Coast* and the 2014 Editor's Prize from *Spoon River Poetry Review.*

A MERE FLASK POURED OUT

Diane Williams

From *Tin House*, Vol. 15, No. 3, Spring 2014

The heavily colored area—it needed to get a shade dingier—after I knocked over her decanter.

There was the sourish smell of the wine and the wine was forcibly—quickly—entering the white linen table covering.

I saw Mother reaching toward the spill, but the time that was left to her was so scant as to be immaterial.

The little incident of the accidental spill had the fast pace of a dreadful race, hitherto neglected or unknown.

"Go home!" Mother said. And I didn't look so good to her she said. "How dare you tell me what to do—when you threw me away! You threw your brother away, too!"

I started hectically to depart and within a month, Mother was dead.

I inherited her glass carafe with its hand-cut, diamond-and-fan design, which we now use on special occasions.

Pouring and serving—we are doing well and we've accomplished many excellent things.

"Don't do it that way!" I had cried. My daughter Maud was attempting to uncork a bottle of wine, but since I thought it was my turn, I took it from her.

Here are other methods I use to apply heavy pressure: I ask Maud where she is going, what does she want, how does she know and why. She should increase her affectionate nature, be successful and happy. Mentally, she must show me she has that certain ability to try.

•

DIANE WILLIAMS is the author of eight books of fiction, and is described by Jonathan Franzen as being "one of the true living heroes of the American avant-garde." Her new story collection—*Fine, Fine, Fine, Fine, Fine*—is due out from McSweeney's in January 2016. She is the editor of the literary annual *NOON*.

AT HOME WITH RAPPER'S DELIGHT

Chris L. Terry

From *tNY.Press*, November 19, 2014

Rapper's Delight didn't feel out of place at school because there were a lot of other people with apostrophes in their names—Ju'Juan, De'Andre, Moni'que. He graduated in 1997, with the honor of being the very last person to finish without email.

His father was a disco song. His mother was a bunch of ideas stolen from other people. But to invoke his parents is to deny that he has studied his past, looking for the version that will shake out the problems as it ripples forward.

Now, it's 2001, and MCs have stopped talking about how funky their beat is and giving shout-outs at the end of a song. They don't even call themselves MCs anymore. Rapper's Delight constantly feels like he's on the phone with someone who launched into talking without saying, "What's up."

On TV, there's a video with a guy sticking his head out of an army tank and shouting. Rapper's Delight grimaces and switches the channel to an old sitcom, the fuzzy screen comforting, the actors' clothes soothing earth tones. This ticks off his friend The Message, who was born in 1982.

Blue smoke rockets from The Message's nose as he passes the blunt across the couch, chasing it with a look of contempt.

"But you don't remember the '70s, R.D. You were born in '79. You ain't even started walking 'til the '80s."

Rapper's Delight is spidering his fingertips through the quarter inch of waves at the top of his fade, willing it to pop out into a 'fro. After a couple beats, he says, "I could even see me at CBGB, wearing leather pants and a necktie with no shirt."

The Message says, "Acting like you remember *Good Times* reruns don't make you some sorta '70s baby."

The Message clicks the remote and the TV show squeezes down to dark. Rapper's Delight looks through the open window, past the power lines and into the night sky, where grainy images flash as he tries to decide what part of the '70s he identifies with most: *Playboy*'s long-form journalism? Baseball players with hair skirting their hats? The contrast between urban blight and bicentennial patriotism that decimated all remaining hippie idealism? *Shaft in Africa?*

His eyes move to the TV, remembering his favorite episode of *Living Single*, where Khadijah and Regine's mothers come to visit and the whole cast breaks into an old rap song about eating a lousy meal.

The macaroni soggy, the peas all mushed and the chicken taste like wood.

Now, *Living Single* is old. Is Rapper's Delight? He crosses the room and bends over the turntable, snatches of music puffing from the speakers as he skips the needle around, trying to find the verse from *Living Single*. The Message rolls his eyes and gets up for the restroom. The song passes in bits and pieces, but the verse has vanished through the grooves. Rapper's Delight is buoyed as his thoughts grind, spark, and about face. His past is falling away, chunk by chunk, leaving only the now and the future.

•

CHRIS L. TERRY's debut novel *Zero Fade* (Curbside Splendor) was on Best of 2013 lists by *Kirkus Reviews*, *Slate Magazine*, and the American Library Association. Chris lives in Los Angeles with his wife and son. Find more of his short stories online in *PANK*, *Hobart*, *SmokeLong Quarterly*, and *Chicago Reader*.

CHICKEN DANCE

Misty Shipman Ellingburg

From *100 Word Story*, March 23, 2014

A 100 Word Story

I went to the exhibit; I met everyone in U of I's Indigenous drum group and asked their names and Tribal affiliations, stating mine. A handsome singer, a Coeur d'Alene Chicken Dancer, drove me home and told me bad rez jokes, *Blasphemy* by Sherman Alexie on the floor of his beat-up pickup. My, my.

He told me, "You're beautiful; come be beautiful around me."

Later, he fucked me, his intensive thrusting in no way indicative of his dance training, his sweet singing, and I was sorry for it, and dry as the prairies where he danced with all that passion.

•

MISTY SHIPMAN ELLINGBURG is a member of the Shoalwater Bay/Willapa Nation. She is an avid participant in cultural activities, to include Tribal Journeys and Northwest powwows. Her work has been published in *Yellow Medicine Review, Camas Magazine, Split Lip*, and more. She is currently working toward her MFA in Fiction from the University of Idaho, class of 2016.

ALL THAT SMOKE HOWLING BLUE

Leesa Cross-Smith

From *Cheap Pop*, January 2014

The first thing Bo ever said to me was that I had a face like an alarm clock—resplendent enough to wake him up. He and his younger brother, Cash, ran a garage on the shitty side of town. My car was always busted. That's how we met.

Since then I'd been living with both of them—driving Bo's old truck whenever I wanted and kissing Cash when Bo was at work. Bo knew about the kissing, I just didn't do it in front of him. I slept in Bo's bed most nights unless he really pissed me off. I loved them both equally. I used to make a peanut butter and jelly joke about it but no one understood what I meant. Bo kept his shoulder-length hair slicked back and Cash kept his short. See? They were different.

Bo had been teaching the blue-eyed shepherd puppy to howl and that's what they were both doing—sitting on the floor, howling at the ceiling. Bo was picking leftover bits of tobacco from his tongue and I reminded him again that he shouldn't smoke in the house. My hair was still scented with woodsmoke from the fire we made out back the night before. Bo stood and stuck his nose against my neck and sniffed me real good. I was at the stove stirring the baked beans.

"Mercy," he said. Soft. It was the name my mama had given me and he always said it a lot. It made me feel special how it got both meanings coming from his mouth. My name, a begging blue prayer. We kissed. Bo's kisses were feathery, Christmas-sweet. Cash hungry-kissed like a soldier on leave.

Bo stuck the puppy underneath his arm and stepped outside. I watched him through the screen, howling up at the sky. The puppy was licking his face.

Cash came through the front door and gently kicked my boots aside to make a path.

"I thought it was my night to make dinner," he said, clinking a six-pack on the kitchen counter.

"You can tomorrow. I made fried chicken, potatoes, and baked beans. Biscuits are in the oven. I got Bo to open the can since it scares me so bad when it pops," I said.

"Well at least he's good for something, right?" Cash said, barely laughing.

"He's out back teaching the puppy to be an asshole," I said, pointing with the wooden spoon, careful not to drip.

"Will you cut my hair tonight?" Cash asked, taking off his ball cap and opening a beer.

"Why? You got a crush on some girl you wanna look cute for?" I asked.

"Yep. Some girl named Mercy," he said, smiling. I twinkled.

The sunset light ached at the windows. The puppy let out a brushy itty-bitty howl that went on forever. It just kept right on crackling. I'm telling you, I thought it'd never stop.

•

LEESA CROSS-SMITH is a homemaker. Her story collection *Every Kiss a War* (Mojave River Press) was a finalist for both the Flannery O'Connor Award for Short Fiction and the Iowa Short Fiction Award. She is the editor of a literary magazine called *WhiskeyPaper* and lives in Kentucky with her husband and babies.

THE INTENDED

Dawn Raffel

From *No Tokens*, Issue 2, Fall/Winter 2014

The babies were in the machines in there, pristine under metal.

The crowd pressed ahead.

"Will you look at them now," he said to me.

I looked at him. His damp brow. Dark eyes. The face filled with something other than wonder, it seemed to me. Rebuke, perhaps. Or grief. Maybe grief, come to think of it. The cut of the hair. A shadow, arid, under the flesh, the angle of the jaw that was familiar to me.

We had been here before—the hall, the lines, the birth of incubation, thrall of the heat. I thought everyone had, that second summer of the fair. The air smelled of perfume, of molten gardenia, and also of stains.

There was a woman selling salt.

The babies were stirring ever so slightly, underneath the instruments, each in isolation.

"Imagine," he said.

Weight, breath: The nurses were jotting all the necessary measurements.

I, of course, agreed with him, although I did not know what to imagine.

Oh, what a fair! You have not seen the like, I can promise you that. Halfway to 1935, July in a curdle. The skyride over the whole of the lakefront. Lights, sweets. The jewel on my finger. The heart of Chicago beating in the water, the world beneath our feet. We walked and walked. Kraft, Ford, Goodyear. The great halls of Science, of Travel and Transport; the Hall of Religion. Out on the midway, a palace of freaks. That poor young girl with eight wild limbs, as if she had another person in her body, craving escape. A fortress intended only for show. In the hot Streets of Paris, the scandalous dancer, Sally Rand—for us, only rumor. A taste in our mouths. A house that was constructed of prefabricated elements.

Milk. Ice.

The grand planetarium, catcher of starlight—the light of the past—was built for us.

And yet it was this: the babies, for whom we stood, we all stood—the coiled line made faint with heat.

The Havoline thermometer registered a record.

"Impossible," he said, meaning maybe just the opposite. Lungs unformed; the seen veins. And still they were breathing.

His hand was on my arm, in a manner of possession or possibly distress.

The doctor intended to save them all: these dreamers, translucent; these citizens in ovens.

Sailor, baker, mother, lover, captain of industry.

What were the odds?

Did I say that I was to marry this man?

We looked and then walked. It was required of us, and there was everybody waiting.

●

DAWN RAFFEL is the author of four books, including two collections of very short stories: *In the Year of Long Division* and *Further Adventures in the Restless Universe*. Her next book, *The Strange Case of Dr. Couney* (due out from Blue Rider/Penguin), is a biography of the above story's incubator doctor on the boardwalk.

YOU WILL EXCUSE ME

George Choundas

From *The Los Angeles Review*, Vol. 15, Spring 2014

He washes his hands. He has shaken a lot of them.

He dries his hands. The backs of them, too.

Really he takes his time washing to put off what follows. He knows this but does it anyway.

Each time the restroom door opens, the sounds rush in. A broad and liquid hum, cocktail glasses, a woman laughing. Bells floating on ocean.

When he goes, he does not have to wait. Immediately it runs red.

It used to be a flecking. A light intermittent pinking. The first time, it was a flecking for a long while before it ran red. Back when it was a mere concern, a curiosity even. A dashboard threatening to peel. A neighbor's porch with one newspaper too many.

Now, in the mornings, sometimes it is still a flecking. Maybe that is not true.

When he was young, he liked to roil every part of the surface. The stream made continents of foam when passed over clear water. Passed over these continents the same stream destroyed them.

Last time it did not go so quickly to red, last time. Before he understood it was something.

One adulthood and how many mailing addresses later and he had forgotten about continents. No room between conference calls for continents.

In the mornings it is more than a flecking, a very generous flecking, but still. It has not entirely turned color, after all. It is not as bad as that.

When they told him it had come back he did not show surprise, did not act like much.

A frizzy sensation at the tip now. Nothing to do with pathology. Just physics. A garden hose at full force, put to the skin, will astonish with how much of a thing, mere material, subject to other things, a person is.

She was at the kitchen table with her glasses on. He was proud of how calmly he told her. His eyes were calm gleams in his face, he made sure of that.

The first time it was a young doctor, vibrating with chatter and optimism. This second one is older. This second one breathes through his nose, slowly, deliberately. He can hear this man breathe against himself when he looks down to write things. Battle-hardened, for a hard battle, for hardly a battle.

When strafed, the continents actually bleed now. No game in that.

At least the doctor did not smile when he said it. Doctors that old can say what they like. "The only guarantee," this one said, "is there are no guarantees."

Briefly, briefly, but he saw it, she looked at the back of her hand after he told her, she looked there before she looked up at him, the same hand she favors to muss his hair and muss it back, the hand that gripped his ear in a light twist as they came out of their first kiss and her saying, "Now remember that when it's time to call me," that tap-tapped the other when he produced the ring but forgot to put it on, that he grasped while she squatted otherwise unassisted over a bedpan after the epidural ("Never seen that in twenty years," said the nurse, "and I been doing this twenty years"), that he held at his brother's funeral and put over his eyes like a blindfold as he bent away from her so she could not see and of course she saw. Before she looked back up at him.

The same stream. It destroys because it's the second time around.

Had that old doctor smiled while saying it he might have smashed in that sagging mouth.

He does not remember it going to red so quickly. The time before.

He washes his hands. He dries his hands. The backs of them, too.

He knows it but he does it anyway. Really he takes his time washing to put off what follows.

The restroom door opens. He goes back to the people, those sounds, these faces, and pretends there are good things in store.

•

GEORGE CHOUNDAS has fiction and nonfiction appearing or forthcoming in over thirty-five publications including *The Southern Review*, *Michigan Quarterly Review*, *The American Reader*, *Mid-American Review*, and *Subtropics*. His stories have been featured as *Longform.org* and *Paragraph Shorts* selections. He is winner of the New Millennium Award for Fiction, is a former FBI agent, and is half Greek and half Cuban.

SCALE

Michael Martone

From *Pleiades*, Vol. 34, No. 1, Winter 2014

SCALE

From the air, the world, falling away below, grew so small. It always struck Art Smith, The Bird Boy of Fort Wayne, how diminished, how minuscule the people in the crowds of people who had come to see him fly became as he climbed. They shrank. Or, more exactly—collapsed, flattened, contracted. Even evaporated. Boiled down to nothing. He was aware of this and other optical illusions flying created. The forced perspective of this new kind of distance was proof that human eyes were not built to see clearly under such circumstances. Our eyes were not like those of the raptors, who could glimpse and target the smallest of the small growing smaller as they soared.

This effect never failed to amaze his passengers back in the early days of exhibition flying. Those observers would have been lucky to have climbed as high as the rooftop of a five-story building or the belfry of a church steeple. They squealed through the prop wash and roar of the engine, "Look, look!" their shouts scrambled and shushed. They gestured instead, squeezing the air between their closing fingers to pinch upon the ever-compressing image of a shrinking spectator below.

SCALE

The war over, Paul Guillow went on to found the company that to this day bears his name. Guillow manufactures model kits of actual aircraft as well as simple penny gliders that when thrown with their pliant wooden wings warped to the proper degree perform rudimentary aeronautic maneuvers, barrel rolls and loops, as they sail through the air. Guillow engaged his former barracks mate and fellow tontine subscriber, Art Smith, to compose, in sky writing, advertising for the new company. Above Wakefield, Massachusetts, in 1925, Art Smith experimented, constructing the message, scaled scales, careful to retrace the schematic he had drawn, *S C A L E,* on a piece of gridded paper onto an unruled sky. From the ground, his airplane was but a mere speck in the heavens, a pinpoint, the nib of an invisible pen from which the letters billowed forth and then disappeared in an invented distance.

SCALE

After all these years of "sky writing" it was still difficult for Art Smith to judge how his compositions appeared to the earthbound onlooker. From where he sat, he was lost in a maze of his own invention. He counted out the seconds during the long reach of an "l," to the point where he felt the stroke should be stopped. The curves and arches and loops were more difficult to produce. He must hold a banking turn while monitoring his compass as it swung through the wide arch of bearings. In the midst of a witty sentiment, he was entangled and enveloped by the clouds, the fog, he himself had generated.

SCALE

Your eyes can play tricks on you. They seem not to be calibrated to see, to comprehended size over great distance, a perspective now made readily possible by heavier-than-air powered flight. Art Smith would, the next year, mistake a light in a farmyard for the lights of the landing strip in Toledo. One night, he found in the depths of one pocket of his flight jacket a newly minted dime whose obverse bore the profile of Liberty in a winged cap though widely mistaken as portraiture of Mercury, the messenger god. He drew it out, and, out of his pocket, the dime's silvered surface caught a flash of moonlight. That clear night, flying with the full moon riding on his wing tip, Smith eyed the planetary heft of that moon muscling into the sky and then, like that, he held up the coin, the thin little wafer tweezed between his fingers, held it at arm's length, and saw it blot out any inkling of another nearby world in all that nearby closing darkness.

CROSSWORD

Michael Martone

From *Ghost Town*, Vol. 5, Issue 1, January 20, 2014

In Nara, Art Smith, The Bird Boy of Fort Wayne, was introduced to aviatrix Katherine Stinson, The Flying School Girl, by General Nagaoka, the imperial impresario who had organized the visits, when their separate demonstration tours of Japan intersected in the soggy city south and west of Tokyo. The citizens of Nara had built a temporary open-sided hangar where the pilots and their aeroplanes took shelter during a steady downpour. Smith returned to Japan with the 1915 model biplane he flew during his first visit. He was very interested in Stinson's craft, a Sopwith biplane, especially its power plant, the Gnome rotary engine salvaged from the wreckage of Lincoln Beachey's fatal crash into San Francisco Bay. The motor had been recovered along with the body. Art recalled witnessing the dead spin into the bay during the Panama-Pacific Exposition. Beachey's monoplane disintegrated, flung hundreds of fractured pieces, flying components, gear, wings all around him. Now here was the very Gnome engine powering Stinson's Pup. What must that somber tableau of the two grounded American flyers inspired in the throng of curious Japanese citizens huddling there, the rain rattling the canvas roof of the hangar? They were the two survivors of the club, including Beachey, that had originated the loop-the-loop. Later, when the weather lifted, the show went on. The two agreed to perform together. Smith rigged a floor oil feed though Stinson's exhaust, allowing her to sky write with him. They took off together, splashing through the rain-soaked field, startling the scattering herds of the heavenly sika deer of Nara as they gained speed. Their coordinated aerial acrobatic maneuvers mirrored the "dog fighting" taking place worlds away. On the ship passage to the East this time, Art Smith had been distracted by the back issues of the *New York World* newspaper in the ship's stateroom and the new puzzle it featured called "Word-Cross," where clues led the contestant to enter letters into blank squares of a diamond-shaped template. He was frustrated, however, discovering that most of the puzzles had been solved, the letters left in their spaces by the thoughtlessness of previous readers. Katherine Stinson was also familiar with the new puzzle craze and was eager to contribute to the simultaneous composition. The "O" hinge, created as the two circled each other elegantly over and over, confused the gaping crowd gazing up from below. Who was the pursued and who the pursuer?

•

MICHAEL MARTONE was born in Fort Wayne, Indiana, the home, then, of Eckrich Meats. Martone (author of *Four for a Quarter*, *Michael Martone*, and *The Blue Guide to Indiana*) ate sandwiches constructed with Eckrich cold cuts: Bologna, Old Fashioned Loaf, Olive Loaf, Honey Loaf, and Pickle & Pimento Loaf. As Martone chewed, he hummed the famous Eckrich jingle: *Talk about good as good can be / it's Eckrich with a big, big E*. And, then, swallowed.

BANANA

Hiromi Kawakami

Translated by Ted Goossen

From *Monkey Business International*, Issue 4, 2014

Uncle Red Shoes always looked worried.

Not just his shoes but his trousers were invariably bright red. His head was clipped from the top of his ears down, while the hair above that was stiffened with gel so that it stood up in spikes.

Though his footwear was always the same identical red, the style varied: sometimes he wore shoes, sometimes lace-up boots, and, depending on the season, beach sandals.

It seemed Uncle Red Shoes had not always lived in our neighborhood.

"I heard that he used to manage a big factory in western Honshu," said the woman who ran the Love, the tiny restaurant-cum-pub.

That factory apparently manufactured stuffed toy eels. Hoping to ride the wave of popularity for Miss Huggie, the black blow-up doll, his father had launched a new stuffed toy, a soft rabbit named Mr. Bunny, which did well (though not as well as Miss Huggie), and followed that in quick succession with Mr. Froggie, Puppykins (which smelled like an actual dog), and finally Mr. Banana, whose skin could be peeled off and stuck back on. All scored a hit with the buying public.

"But the factory went bankrupt after he took over, and he came here," she continued.

Uncle Red Shoes always sang the song "Hardly Worth a Confession" when he visited her pub, which drove her absolutely nuts.

"I mean, that's one of my signature songs!" she said.

People thought that the reason Uncle Red Shoes was so worried might be the financial problems he was having with the dance studio he had opened five years back.

"What sort of dance does he teach there?" I asked.

"How the heck should I know? The Banana Dance, perhaps?"

Whenever I passed Uncle Red Shoes on the street, something good was sure to happen the next day. Last time I picked up a five-hundred-yen coin. The time before that I won a bottle of cooking wine at a raffle held by the local shops. And the time before that I was the one who got picked up. "Join me for a cup of tea?" the man said, and by the end he had bought me twelve packs of fried noodles and given me ten back issues of *Shōnen Jump*.

Uncle Red Shoes lived on the third floor of the dance studio. Every once in a while he danced on the street. Raising one leg in the air, he twirled around and around—I've seen him spin as many as five times.

"You know what that dance is called?" Midori Kawamata asked me when we were hanging out together.

"The Banana Dance?" I replied, but she just shot me a dirty look.

"No, that's the *grand fouetté*."

Not long after that, the dance studio went bankrupt. The first floor was turned into a second location for the Love pub and the second floor rented out as office space, but Uncle Red Shoes continued to live on the third floor, where he remains to this day. I sometimes see him dancing the *grand fouetté* on the street. He looks awfully worried, but his twirls are gorgeous.

•

HIROMI KAWAKAMI is one of Japan's leading novelists. Among her prizes are the Akutagawa Prize, the Woman Writer's Prize, the Tanizaki Prize, and the Yomiuri Literature Prize. Counterpoint Press has published two of her books: *Manazuru*, translated by Michael Emmerich in 2010 (Japan–U.S. Friendship Commission Prize), and *The Briefcase*, translated by Allison Markin Powell in 2012.

TED GOOSSEN teaches humanities at York University in Toronto, Canada. He is the editor of *The Oxford Book of Japanese Short Stories* and is presently coeditor, with Motoyuki Shibata, of *Monkey Business International*, the first Japanese literary magazine available in an English version. He has translated a number of Japanese writers, including Naoya Shiga, Hiromi Kawakami, and Haruki Murakami.

OBJECTS OF DESIRE

Adam O'Fallon Price

From *Narrative Magazine*, Fall 2014

AN iSTORY

Hopelessly in love, and going crazy as a virginal bachelor nearing thirty, Xin Bao had gotten drunk and stolen a hyacinth macaw to give the girl as a gift. It was a long story, but basically: he wanted her, she wanted the bird, there you had it. Last night the storefront glass on the ground around him had twinkled with merry, sinister approval at his boldness.

This morning he awoke with a dreadful hangover, the cage in the corner dashing his fleeting, solitary hope that it had all just been a dream. The bird squawked at his approach, seeming to repeat *jail! jail! jail!* The girl, he knew, would report him. He opened the window and the cage and watched the blue-green-yellow blur darting back and forth among the gray apartment towers, diving then ascending on invisible spires of hot chimney air, in utter disbelief at its own good fortune.

•

ADAM O'FALLON Price's stories have appeared, or will soon appear, in *The Paris Review*, *The Iowa Review*, *Narrative Magazine*, *Glimmer Train*, and *The Mid-American Review*, among others. His debut novel, *Gravity's Gone*, will be published by Doubleday in 2016.

ANNABEL

Lauren Becker

From *If I Would Leave Myself Behind: Novella and Stories*
(Curbside Splendor, 2014)

Annabel was cracked where no one could see. Hairline, but beneath. She waited for one of them to feel it. To say something. They never said.

She looked whole, which satisfied. Annabel wore cardigans with jeans, black or white tanks beneath. Slight hints of things. The unbuttoning of the sweater sacred. For them.

Her purse was brown. A name stitched on it. Not hers. Her name unusual enough that they had not met another. Most could spell it. In emails and texts where they said the things they couldn't. Mouths too greedy to spell the things she needed. They did not need those things. She stopped asking.

The crack came in seventh grade, when the chemistry teacher she worshipped, worshipped back. He offered her time alone, something she did not get. Working parents. Brother with Down's syndrome. They cared for him and sleepwalked the remainder of their awake hours. They gave her the name and soon had nothing left. She missed them like a distant season.

Annabel, he breathed, as he gave her more work, more instruction. He stood over her and gave her his attention.

She took it. She gave back. She could not tell.

She told her secrets on paper and hid them. Nobody looked. Her retarded brother went through her things, looking for candy, not knowing how to enter and leave without fingerprints. She left chocolate bars and candy necklaces under her pillow. He left his imprint and wrappers on her bedspread. She slept curled in his rounded outline.

"Peter," she whispered, in his ear, while he watched cartoons. "Can you see it? The crack?" He smacked at her with his limp hand and demanded a bowl of cereal. Annabel brought him cereal and watched him eat. She had mostly stopped, four years before, when she lost interest in chemistry.

The teacher left her messages, still. He sent her letters. Annabel. Please. She recognized his attention now as a lure for theft. She ignored him and met men at gas stations and coffee shops. They thought she was in college. She was older than her history. They admired her name. They felt her hipbones beneath them and called it. She stopped waiting.

She traded the name for Ann. She began to study chemistry again.

Ann started college, leaving behind relieved parents and candy, hidden with simple maps for her brother. She took the paper, weighty, along with towels and books and cardigan sweaters. She left the crack and made herself whole.

It addressed itself in a letter she opened. She accepted it, familiar in the unknown place. Addressed to Annabel, she named herself familiar, too.

·

LAUREN BECKER is editor of *Corium Magazine*. Her work has appeared in *Tin House, American Short Fiction, The Los Angeles Review, Juked, Wigleaf,* and elsewhere. This story appeared in different form in *PANK* in Winter 2011.

THE BOY AND THE BEAR

Blake Kimzey

From *Families Among Us* (Black Lawrence Press, 2014)

The boy woke in the forest, covered in snow, and blinked at the nickel-sized flurries falling on his face. He looked closely at his forearms and hands: dark black hair, brittle as icicles, and claws that shone like dull bone. He lay under the hangover of a jagged stand of rocks near the banks of a river carrying drift ice southward. A large black bear had its snout near the boy's face, its breath warm and wet. Wind blew snow from the shoulders of tall pines on either side of the river and cracking wood echoed through the forest.

The boy focused on the bear before him and didn't move. The boy was cold, his nose frozen with ice that cleaved as he drew in full, waking breaths. His lungs burned with the deepness of his breathing. The boy couldn't remember how long he had been asleep, hibernating. When he entered the forest months ago, a chill hung in the air and the mountains loomed beyond the balding tree limbs. Now everything was white, bits of brown peeking through at the base of trees and where outsized boulders broke through the powder. The boy had run from his village until he was lost among the pines and small earthen dens that pockmarked the hard packed ground. That was some time ago. His arms and legs had been covered in a soft down of fur then, as if a watercolorist had put the boy on an easel and gone to work detailing every hair.

As he looked at the bear the boy thought of his parents. His mother and father had locked him in the root cellar after his ears grew pointed and his teeth became too long and sharp for his mouth to contain. They said they wouldn't feel safe with a bear living in the house, not after his brother had roared forth from their front door four years before and pawed through the village before being shot near the church, which anchored the village, its white steeple rising skyward to the lightning rod atop the wooden cross. His brother continued toward the thick wood leaving a trail of blood and disappeared into the dense summer foliage.

Four years later, as if overnight, the boy showed signs of changing like his older brother: first a curved back and an inclination to walk on all fours, and then a deep growling voice that sunk low on hard consonants. Finally, in late October, his father manhandled him outside with the moon high overhead. All the boy could do was growl and swipe at the air in front of him. They struggled against each other. The father covered the boy's mouth with his hand, which smelled strongly of pork and dirt. His father's arms were round with muscle from working the fields, plowing rows, seeding corn and wheat, wrestling livestock. The boy was not yet big enough to challenge his father and he went quickly into the cellar, worked his way down the mud-speckled steps and looked over his shoulder as his father latched the door shut. He let out a growl that hurt his ears in the small space of the cellar, which held the scent of mildew, dusty cornhusks, and discarded bits of wheat chaff.

The boy watched the village from a slit in the cellar door. Gray smoke billowed from tin-capped chimneys on thatched roofs. Women and girls carried pails of water from a stone-lined well, boys chopped wood, and men led teams of oxen into fields ringing the village, all of them preparing for the cold that would soon grip the valley. The boy's mother chanced a visit once, held her palm to the latch on the cellar door and blocked what light bled through the cracks. The boy heard her whimpering, or she could have been humming a hymn. The lightness of her voice was stolen in the crisp air rushing through the village. The boy cried out to his mother, but by then his voice was deep and startling. She turned quickly, held up the hem of her dress, and rushed to the small house where the boy knew she would prep a stew or pot roast, her delicious bread certainly ready for the oven.

The cellar was cold and damp. The dusting of hair that covered the boy's body kept him warm. When he looked down he saw a snout taking shape in the middle of his face, wet and dark-colored in the dim light. The boy's clothes were tight and the leather of his boots dug into his feet, so painful he had to take them off. It took a week, but the boy used his claws and the tip of his snout to dig out from the cellar. He emerged under the wall abutting the edge of the forest and fled unnoticed in the middle of the night. The boy ran toward the mountains until he was lost and tired, panting like an animal.

With the bear looking over him, the boy rose steadily until he was firmly on all fours. He felt like a statue, his coat of fur matted and frozen; bending his knees felt like breaking through a thin vein of stone. The boy and the bear stood nose to nose, their breath suspended like mist between them. The bear's right ear was half missing and his right eye had the rheumy blue glaze of an old man's cataract. The bear licked the boy's face and then turned to walk along the bank of the river; he occasionally pawed at the thick winter water. The bear had a hitch in his gait, and the boy followed closely behind. They continued into the forest and night fell. The boy followed the bear's tracks under a full moon until they found a home deep in the thick wood, and in time he thought of the village no more.

•

BLAKE KIMZEY graduated from the MFA Programs in Writing at UC Irvine in 2014 and is the recipient of a generous Emerging Writer Grant from The Elizabeth George Foundation. His fiction has been adapted for broadcast on NPR and published by *Tin House, McSweeney's, Green Mountains Review, FiveChapters, The Lifted Brow, Puerto del Sol, The Los Angeles Review, Short Fiction, PANK, Fiction Southeast, The Masters Review*, and anthologized in *Surreal South '13*. Kimzey recently completed his first novel, and his chapbook of short tales, *Families Among Us*, won the 2013 Black River Chapbook Competition and was published by Black Lawrence Press.

SOMETHING OVERHEARD

Yennie Cheung

From *decomP magazinE*, December 2014

The walls of your apartment are as thin as the girl next door. She's nineteen and a model from Slovakia or Slovenia or some other European country you couldn't place on a map. The two of you don't talk, and you tell people it's because she doesn't speak much English, which is true. But you suspect the bigger problem is that you don't speak a word of Versace.

Your roommate, Sunny, is fluent in Louis Vuitton, but they don't talk much, either. Sunny is offended that the girl never smiles, never even nods a greeting when they pass each other on the stairs. Comparatively, you and model girl are best friends. Once, when you saw her by the mailboxes, you smiled and said hello. She covered her eyes with her oversized sunglasses and mumbled what you assumed was a greeting but to your ears sounded vaguely like "Rutabaga."

You always know when the neighbor is at home because, as Sunny puts it, she marks her territory like an anorexic greyhound. On evenings when she smokes on her balcony, you smell it through the windows, and the scent lingers on your Ikea drapes. On afternoons, you hear her through the air-conditioning vents, usually laughing over the phone and saying things that sound like "Machu Picchu" or "Dostoyevsky." Sunny assures you the girl has heard of neither.

On weekends, the neighbor turns up her aerobics DVD, and the walls tremble like a big rig in your blind spot. The first time it happened, you ducked under a table for fear of the bookshelves toppling over.

"I don't understand," you said. "She weighs, like, nothing."

Sunny sniffed. "Runway models. All they ever do is stomp."

The neighbor does more than runways, though. You know this because you saw her in a magazine once. She was sitting with her back to the camera, wearing nothing but an expensive silver watch, her head turned demurely to the side and her lips slightly parted. Your first reaction was to wonder what a naked teenager had to do with selling watches.

But when you looked more carefully, your breath caught, because the curve of her hips and the downward glance of her eye were somehow exquisite. Earnest. As if she were incapable of disguising herself. You told yourself that she was Photoshopped or something. That it seemed impossible for these sensuous hips to be the same flat, brittle things you'd seen stalking up the stairwell in platform heels and skinny jeans. That this couldn't be the same eye that once took in the dirt on your sneakers and the thickness of your thighs and turned away.

Tonight, as you arrive home from work, you hear a deep, trembling bray coming from her apartment. You assume that she is on the phone, laughing, but as you slide your key into the lock you stop. You hear her choke. You hear her sob. She strains for composure but moans so terribly that you're both heartbroken for her pain and ashamed for being fascinated by it.

You turn the deadbolt to your door slowly so she can't hear you coming home. She is louder inside your apartment, her voice tinny through the air vents. As you curl onto the couch and listen, you realize that you know this sound— that you've seen this pain. It is your father sprawled over your mother's casket. It is your roommate, watching a tsunami destroy her homeland. It is you, watching that gold band slide across the coffee table as the love of your life says, "I can't do this. Not anymore."

Now, with your curiosity defeated, you pull your knees to your chest. You wrap your arms around them as if you are holding your neighbor's bony shoulders. It would be easy to walk next door and perform this small act of consolation in person, but you can't. You shouldn't. You won't. You know that what she's doing is more personal than the contours of her body, as intimate as sex. Who are you to intrude on this moment? You are just a neighbor—a stranger. Who are you to understand her sorrow, as if it were that commonplace, that *pedestrian*? You can't do that to her. So you will let her grieve. She has the right to feel that this pain is singular—that this is a language no one else can speak.

•

Yennie Cheung holds an MFA in Creative Writing from UC Riverside–Palm Desert. Her work has been published in such places as the *Los Angeles Times* and *Word Riot*. A native of Southern California, she is currently working on a book of nonfiction about Downtown Los Angeles.

THE LUNAR DEEP

David Mellerick Lynch

From *The Stinging Fly*, Spring 2014

My old dad, as his wits weighed anchor, decreed himself a
Noah of the still and the dead and went about with a note-
pad cataloguing stones and stars and other bleak insensate
things that they might be redeemed, at Judgement Day, from
the final deluge of obscurity. It was a job of slow and rococo
care but a man should, after all, enjoy the ballast of a hobby
in his decline.

"Sea of Serenity," he said. "Sea of Tranquillity. Seas of
Moisture, of Islands, of Rain."

He sketched snail shells and twigs and the texture of
the interstellar satin. He compared the flavours of pebbles.
He learned, in a book, the rules of sonnets, apostrophising
the quintessence of the dust on the mantelpiece, the his-
tories hidden in the skins of petrified worms. Some of the
neighbours thought he was a grand fellow. They engaged
him by lawns and lampposts in disquisitions on the project, examining his records, stroking their chins. Certain
nude excursions rendered the rest of them aghast and my
mother confined him to the garden shed, where for hours
daily he scribbled, scissored, classified, mused, compiled.

As he lay one morning in the spread wings of his dressing-
gown, watching the moon's frail shirked husk cling, falter,
and submit to sheer blue, he determined—purple-cheeked,

dew-silvered—to become a student of Diana, eternally. He bought a telescope from Lidl. He began to haunt the nights, or point across his picked-at dinner in the winter evenings, bid me turn and, trailing a fingertip across the window, name the basalt fields that bruised the hanging face, the *oceanus* and *maria*, the *laci* and *pali* and *sini*.

"Sea of Clouds. Sea of Crisis. And that big one, the Ocean of Storms."

If I called him a fucking lunatic he seemed not to get the joke. He arrived at the door once on the arm of a Guard, nodding at me whenever the breeze in the dressing-gown uncovered the brush of grey wire and balls like diver's leads, and my mother took her glasses off, turning away. For a while he went on all fours, like a werewolf, and though I considered this appropriate I felt bad for my mother, who coughed raggedly, or cried in the bathroom, and I began to hate him, and it didn't help that he started forgetting where to put the milk or find his hat or how to work the telescope or what my mother's name was, what was her name for Christ's sake, the slut the bloody bitch she'll smother me with my pillow while I sleep you'll see. But it placated him to be asked about the moon.

"Sea of Fertility. Sea of Nectar."

After death, he said, he wished to be flown by unmanned probe to the deepest crater on the dark side and laid out in his dressing-gown, there to crumble peacefully to lunar dust.

"Sea of Cold."

We scattered his ashes in a dried-out rockpool.

•

DAVID MELLERICK LYNCH is from Cork City in Ireland. He is a graduate in English from Trinity College, Dublin, and is currently getting his bearings in the hostile country of the Real World. His fiction has appeared in *Icarus*, *The Stinging Fly*, *Three Monkeys Online*, and the *Irish Times*.

ANGLE

Roland Leach

From *Apeiron Review*, Issue 6, Spring 2014

I only knew an angle of my father. An acute angle. A tiny slice that changed from where you stood. I sometimes caught him in the corner of my eye and thought, that's him. Getting out of his truck, dirty from work, pine resin on his arm hair, black oil across his face. Or in the Chrysler with the kids singing.

Never was.

I tried to look in the wrong direction, hoping he had left something of himself. Just a trace, so had I been a sniffer-dog I could have tracked him.

But he was light-footed, shadowless.

He came home every day but was never there, came home every day with his one trick of disappearing into light.

•

ROLAND LEACH has four collections of poetry, the latest being *My Father's Pigs* (Picaro Press). He is proprietor of Sunline Press, which has published eighteen collections by Australian poets, and his most recent venture is *Cuttlefish*, an art and literary magazine. Leach is a past winner of the Newcastle Poetry Prize and Josephine Ulrick Prize, was the recipient of an Australia Council Grant to write poetry in the Galapagos Islands, and was anthologized in *The Best Australian Poems 2012*.

THE DIRECTOR

Anya Yurchyshyn

From *NOON*, 2014

"We hold your loved ones for a month," the director of the crematory said when he called. "After that, we come for you. We're not like the cleaners."

I went that evening. The different pamphlets that lined the coffee table all had clouds on their covers. I shuffled them, then shuffled them again, but the weather wouldn't change.

The man placed my mother on the counter. I'd selected an urn that could easily be confused for a Chinese vase, but I no longer appreciated that. When I saw it now I thought, This thing is so ugly, and if I screw off the top I will hear my mother scream.

The man gave me a stack of papers and said that one of the most painful things about death was the paperwork. I said I appreciated the structure it provided. He asked what my plans were. I told him I was hoping to rent a small beach house for the summer.

"I meant your plans for your mother," he said. "I'm sure it would be easy to find a place for her. She'd add elegance to any room. Or you could take her away. People often choose to scatter their loved ones in exotic locations."

"OK," I said.

He carried my mother to my car, buckled her to the backseat, and told me how he hated seeing people put their loved ones in the trunk. "It's sealed," he explained as he tightened the seat belt, "but you still don't need her flying around."

I sat in my car and watched two other people retrieve their loved ones. I wondered about my plans.

When I got home I placed my mother next to my waxy plant. Then I went back to the driveway and stared at her and the plant through the casement window.

My mother always seemed surprised when she found herself on the phone with me or in pictures from my childhood. When I was young she used to joke that she was adopted, that I'd somehow adopted her and what could she do?

I should mention here that I am a collector. I have a collection of rose-patterned Chinese porcelain that present, I think, a romantic visual effect.

My mother in the ugly vase and the waxy plant were in the vicinity of some flea market souvenirs from India, the Cape. My floorboards are from a barn down in old Mexico. My bathroom art is provocative.

•

ANYA YURCHYSHYN's first book, an investigative memoir titled *My Dead Parents*, is forthcoming from Crown Publishing. Her writing has been published by *Esquire*, *Granta*, and *N+1*, and she is a frequent contributor to *NOON*.

THE FAMILY JEWEL

Ron Riekki

From *Blue Fifth Review: Blue Five Notebook Series*, May 2014

We have IVs hooked up to each other, back of the ambulance.

We could get fired, but for the amount of liability we have and the little pay we get, who cares.

IV is the quickest hangover cure on the planet. Trust me. If you ever feel like you're dying from a hangover, contact a nurse you know. A medic. An EMT. Anyone who can hook you up with some intravenous cleansing. You feel like a new man. A new man ready to haul around drunks all night.

That's what nights are in L.A. Drunks.

During the day, we take diabetics to dialysis. The overeaters. The hyperglycemic.

At night, the over-drinkers. The over-dosers. The over-overs. The ones wacked out of their heads. And this is L.A. So just imagine how nutty I'm talking about. People who can make a transvestite Captain Jack Sparrow walking in and out of moving highway traffic look like a rather sober thing to do.

We'd just got done with a call. A teen girl needed to go to a psych ward. She said nothing. We bring her in. Room full of girls. Soon as she gets inside, soon as we turn her over, she throws over a table. Like Jesus with the moneylenders. When we had her, calm as a stilled ocean. Then the second I turn over the PCR, she goes ape-crap.

I love those kinds of patients. She could see it in my eyes. That I was drunk. That I live in the hood. That I'm one of hers. Then she gets in with the nurses making quadruple what I make and realizes it's time for them to earn their money.

My partner takes out his IV, moves to the front seat, rogers the call.

Unknown medical.

My favorite call, because it means "anything goes." No idea what we'll step into. I unplug and get passenger side. We're there in minutes. A halfway house. We knock. A guy answers the door. He looks like *Currie*. Every inch of him blood-soaked. They tell you BSI in medic school. Body substance isolation. It means, "Don't get their blood mixed in with yours."

He's an epidural hematoma.

No big deal.

Alcoholics bleed a lot. Because they hit their heads a lot.

I can tell from his LOC, his skin, his airway, his entire demeanor that he's far from shock.

He's drunk and bloody.

It happens.

I tell him to hop on the gurney, we'll take him in.

He says he has to go to his room first.

Fine.

He's got a Buddha statue in his room. Just a bed, lamp, dresser, and plastic obese Buddha. Clothes on the floor. A carpet hanging in the closet.

He says he can't go.

I ask why.

He says he needs to piss on the Buddha.

You need to what?

Buddha-piss.

He pulls it out. You know, *it*.

My partner stands, arms folded. He hates psych patients. Says every drunk is a psych patient. Truth is, he hates all patients.

Half your medics, they're like that.

My advice, if you don't want to roll the dice, end up with a medic who'll kill you, drive yourself to the hospital. Long as you think you can live 'til you get there.

Stage fright, says the patient, I need someone to piss with me.

Can we do that? I ask my partner.

I once pissed on a guy's leg who got stung by a jellyfish.

Right on the beach?

Yeah.

Front of everyone?

There wasn't anybody there. Just him and his friends and they were drunk, thought it was funny.

I motion for him to go ahead.

He shakes his head no.

I say to the patient, if I piss will you go with us, I mean, without any complaints?

No, he says, and starts pissing. Right in the Buddha's face.

The rest of the halfway house is asleep. They don't care what's going on. I'm surprised someone even called 911.

He finishes, shakes, picks up the Buddha, and sits on the gurney with it in his lap.

We wheel him into the ambulance.

My partner drives.

We have a deal—psych patients, he drives. Any patient with an injury to the eye, I drive.

I can't stand eye injuries. We had a fishhook once. Caught deep. The pointy end posterior, into the vitreous humor. That jelly-like drainage made me want to quit the job on the spot.

Instead I made this deal. Not realizing we'd never have another eye call. But half our calls are psych patients. So I've been in the back with a man who kept asking me to stop making rainbows. A senior citizen who tried to rape me. A woman dressed like a werewolf who said she needed to get to Germany or the cowboys would kill her.

In comparison, epidural hematoma seems easy. The Buddha calming him.

I take his vitals. Hypertension, but mild. Tachycardic, mild. Tachypnic, mild. Sometimes it's just the ambulance that causes that. The excitement of the ride.

He says, it's nice what you do.

Which is?

Saving lives.

Yeah, I say, I've saved so many lives.

Tonight we had a sprained ankle and a common cold.

Two lives saved.

He holds the Buddha out. Motions for me to take it.

No, I say, thanks though.

He keeps holding it out.

I tell you what, I say, put it over there. He'll be the new ambulance Buddha.

Everyone should have an ambulance Buddha, he says. No one will ever die in the presence of an ambulance Buddha.

We get to the hospital, drop him off, and go back to decontaminate. Rub down the gurney. Antiseptic towelettes. Takes a minute.

Partner sees the Buddha.

I tell him the patient didn't forget it, that it's ours now.

He says to throw it away, that it's gotta be filled with bacteria.

Urine sterilizes, I say.

Not enough. Throw it out.

We stare at it. It stares at us. Piss in its eyes.

•

Ron Riekki's books include *U.P.: a novel; The Way North: Collected Upper Peninsula New Works* (Wayne State University Press, selected by the Library of Michigan as a 2014 Michigan Notable Book); and *Here: Women Writing on Michigan's Upper Peninsula* (Michigan State University Press). His play *Carol* was included in *The Best Ten-Minute Plays 2012*, and his screenplay *The First Real Halloween* was best sci-fi/fantasy screenplay for the 2014 International Family Film Festival. His poetry, fiction, and nonfiction have been in *Spillway, Prairie Schooner, River Teeth, Juked, decomP, Sundog Lit,* and many other literary journals.

PISTOLS AT TWENTY PACES
On the Last Recorded Duel in Hancock County, Mississippi, April 23, 1866

Michael Garriga

Illustrated by Tynan Kerr

From *The Book of Duels* (Milkweed Editions, 2014)

Philip Lacroix, 51
Colonel, CSA

He robbed me more grossly than Grant, more deeply than Lincoln and these twenty paces pale compared to the one thousand miles and more I walked from that captured officers' camp in Illinois where snow seeped through shoe soles so cold I cut felt from my hat to patch them warm and dry and back home the courthouse burned down—Goddamn Gen'ral Butler, I'd hang him were I the governor—and with it went all the county records—deeds and land titles and all—and my slaves were freed and stole whatall they could carry and after I'd taken such good care of them as God set forth for me in dominion, so this traitor and coward and former friend, who ate of my lunch Sundays after church, could take my lawful owned cattle and claim them for his own, after I branded their hides while my darkies held them still. The smell of torched flesh in my hair and nose, that odor so like a battlefield, while the persistent wind, like this one, blows brittle leaves and cools the sweat burning on my skin and the judge hollers, *Fire*:

I turn and squeeze the stiff trigger—I know I am right in this course and God will prove me true with the aim of my bullet: hot sulfur smell, thick smoke in sunlight, and a snarl of flame like the hell we're both bound for.

Etienne Thigpen, 46
Veteran, U.S. Artillery Division

He come home a fool-headed war hero to judge and insult me. We walked down to the lower field of fresh turned earth—iron and onion and scat—where he accused me of stealing his cows which I had bought clear, got a cash ticket for proof and now I'm sorry I ever prayed for his sorry-ass soul. Sure, I ran some hooch out to the blockade, but that don't make me no damn traitor, just a trader with them boys in blue who gave me coffee—the same chic'ry then as what coats my tongue now—and more, I suffered the hardships of war, boiling sea water to get at the salt to keep my food, and done fought my war too—took a bullet in Mexico with Stuart and Lee and now my sweat-clammy palms wrap 'round this pistol butt, smell horse lather and oil on this iron piece, see them mildewed Spanish moss tendrils come ribboning off oaks slashed by sun beams. Accuse me of stealing and lying to boot, I refute his claim same as I did old Thibideaux's back in '53, may God rest his soul in smoke and flame eternal, *Fire*:

I turn and my hand blooms a white cloud of smoke as though I'm holding a fistful of baby's breath: good gracious, boys, I'm hit and done; please say sweet things of me to Mary.

Mrs. Etienne Thigpen (née Mary Annette Cuevas), 18
Watching Her Husband Duel

From where I crouch behind the pleached crosshatching of azalea branches, I see the two men standing back to back like stuck twins and wonder how they can be that close and not kill each other now—Etienne's face flushed, his shoes, as always, thick with mud, and that preening blowhard, Philip, just as calm as Sunday afternoon, his clothes pressed and his boots polished and shined, prepared for death or murder one, yet it's my hands that rattle these petals from the branches, and beyond them the Gulf catches the sunlight in little spinning coins, like the bright dimples in the cheeks of the Kaintock man who touched my wrist at the Saint Stanislaus social and who, in that moment, bade me run away with him to New Orleans—oh, to stroll along the banquets arm-in-arm under the iron-worked balconies and to eat almond truffles or pralines brought 'round by Creole women wearing bright-colored *tignons* and hoop earrings that brush their bare shoulders like I wish I could wear mine—and we'd attend the Conde Street balls, dancing and sweating under the flambeaux, where we'd glide through the measures of the contredanse or sip wine in the American cabarets until I'd retire to his arms and bed and he could take my ankles and toes in his mouth and I'd take him in mine and he'd not smell like cattle and night soil and I yearn to leave this backwood outhouse, these backward outhouse men, whose petty wars and self-puffery leave me hungry as the war ever did, when I had to parch corn to make coffee till my guts were pulled like the dead girl from my womb whom I buried in secret while Etienne was off making whiskey or God knows what, to walk away as these men here have walked away one from the other but without sense enough between them to know it better to continue to walk and never to turn around as they have turned now—*Fire*:

A twin roaring, two great clouds of smoke, and a scream—I have prayed for this bittersweet moment—the taking of Etienne from me and from life—but in my dreams I am not his little Mary Annette, hiding behind a bush, heart pounding so hard it makes my hands shake, but rather, I am the bullet squeezed from the burning steady barrel, freed.

•

MICHAEL GARRIGA is from the Gulf Coast of Mississippi. His first book, *The Book of Duels,* published by Milkweed Editions and illustrated by Tynan Kerr, captures the final moments of thirty-three duels in flash triptychs, considering each battle from three perspectives. Currently he coedits the online journal *Fiction Southeast* and teaches at Baldwin Wallace University in Berea, Ohio.

TYNAN KERR is a painter, ceramicist, and illustrator living and working in Minneapolis, Minnesota.

LET'S SAY

Julia Strayer

From *SmokeLong Quarterly*, Issue 46, December 15, 2014

Let's say I'm being robbed, but I choose to believe I'm pushing my daughter on the swings in the park across from the Methodist church, autumn leaves collecting on the grass as the wind blows, and with each push she becomes a year older until she's my age and I'm still my age, but she knows more than I do because that's how kids are these days. She knows what we'll have for dinner, that it will rain at eight the next morning and that I'm dying. The robber doesn't mean to shoot, but he's young and twitchy, and I've seen his face. When he planned the whole thing he hadn't thought it through, and thinking on the fly isn't his strong suit. Even his mother knows that much. She told him and told him, as he grew, he'd never amount to anything unless he could learn to think five steps ahead, but he didn't, couldn't, so robbing was one of his only career choices, and he isn't very good at that either so he shoots me in the chest and runs. I look down in disbelief and plug the hole with my thumb trying to remember what I'd touched with that thumb and imagining all the resistant bacteria mobilizing into my bloodstream, and if the bullet didn't kill me the infection surely would. I never told my daughter where the will was or the insurance policy or the secret bank account where I was saving up for something crazy like tightrope lessons or a yearlong driving trip across country from one small-town diner to the next, or to live off the land—put up a windmill, keep chickens and grow our own food, just to see if we could. I want to keep pushing her on the swings, but I don't want her to be older than I am. She'll blame me one day, when she realizes she lost so many years of her childhood from the swings. Yes, she'll be angry. I can already see the anger building in her, little lines spiderwebbing at the edges of her eyes as the detectives try to tell her they're doing the best they can to find the twitchy kid whose mother shakes her head when he gets home with trembling hands and my blood splattered on his T-shirt. And she knows he's done something stupid that can't be undone so she wipes the sweat from her forehead with her handkerchief embroidered with violets, and she sits on the couch to give her heart a chance to slow down so she can catch her breath while his eyes dart around the room and he makes wild gestures, laying out the whole story while I'm still lying on the street wondering if spinning my daughter on the merry-go-round would take off the years the swings put on so she'll be little again like I remember her when she seemed too young to walk home from school by herself, her backpack almost bigger than she was, when she had nothing but opportunity in front of her; I'm thinking the same thoughts the twitchy kid's mother is thinking about her son when he was little, with long dark eyelashes that made the girls follow after him, and she still had hope. And we both play the What-If game, me wondering whether things would be different if I'd stopped at the dry cleaners before the bank, the mom wondering if she should have pushed him more toward sports or the band or the science club and if it would have mattered, if he'd still be standing before her crying about how he shot a woman in the Elm Street parking lot and ran. The mom knows it doesn't matter what she did or didn't once do; it only matters if she sends him to the shower while she burns his clothes with the autumn leaves she raked up and collected in the barrel out back, or whether she picks up the phone.

•

JULIA STRAYER's fiction appears or is forthcoming in *SmokeLong Quarterly* and *Glimmer Train*, where she placed first in the *Glimmer Train* Short Story Award for New Writers. She earned an MFA from Sarah Lawrence College and teaches creative writing at New York University.

EL PASO: JULY

Jeff Streeby

From *Camroc Press Review*, November 2014

Mike is trying to lift up the horse's head and I'm on one knee trying to get at the big vein in the neck. The sorrel's eyes are closed: a week of this and he's almost used up—washy and shaky and about to go down. But before I can open the stop on the jug of Ringer's, he squeals and bawls and is up on his hind legs, backing away. He's like that for what seems a long time before everything stops and he falls over backwards. When he hits the ground, a cloud of red dust rises and his last breath leaves him all at once—a loud choked-off grunt.

Shadows are falling. The sky at this hour is layered in reds—all the shades of chestnut horses. The dust is settling. The morning glories climbing the barn are closing up. Soon the coyotes will be out, the burrowing owls. Nighthawks will be calling.

Mike holds the broken lead shank. I wince at my bloody wounds—shoulder, hip, and head. The dead horse's hide is wet with sweat. We don't move. We don't say a thing.

West Texas sunset—

in the seam of earth and sky,
this hot, still moment.

Maybe we knew all along that he would die, but we were young and did not expect life to surrender with such violent reluctance, did not expect the husk of it lying there in the yard to be so different, so absolutely empty.

•

JEFF STREEBY, a Pushcart Prize nominee and a nominee for *Best of the Net Anthology*, is an old cowboy who earned his MFA in Poetry from Gerald Stern's program at New England College. He is a Senior Lecturer in English at Assumption University of Thailand (ABAC, Bang Na campus) in Bangkok.

YOU MUST INTERCEPT THE BLUE BOX BEFORE IT GETS TO THE CITY

Ron Carlson

From *The Blue Box* (Red Hen Press, 2014)

Get that box! It must not get to the city; everybody knows that. It must be stopped from getting to the city. Go after the box and make sure it does not reach the city. Act quickly and intercept the box before it arrives in the city. Go to the shipping terminal and run through the big warehouse, past the conveyor belts carrying all the packages and boxes and cardboard tubes full of maps. Run! If you see a blue box, check it out. Some will be too small, some too big. Don't be fooled by the other blue boxes. When you see it dumped into the delivery truck, note the truck's number, like if it is seventeen or ninety, some number and pursue that truck. I guess you'll use a motorcycle. Just jump on a motorcycle and chase that truck. The box! Drive ahead of the truck and signal the driver to stop. When you check the back of the truck, all the boxes will be blue! This is bad, and all you can do is turn around and watch the driver run away with one blue box! That is the box you must stop from getting to the city. Chase him on foot, even if he climbs onto the roof of that building. Go up the rain gutter, climbing the way you were trained in your other life, where you were lonely, strong, and sad, and run across the rooftops. When he slips down the Italian tile roof and falls three stories to the ground, quickly climb down the wall using your techniques. Yes, he's dead! Or is he? He could be faking.

Some guys in this spot fake it and lie there. But where is the box? Could it be magnetized to the back wall of the dumpster in the alley by his body? Look there. No, because the box is not magnetic! Quick. Think. How do you stop the blue box from getting to the city? Everyone you love lives in the city. You only love a few people, say three or four, depending. You admire your nephew, he's in the top rank at his institute, but you don't love him. He's annoying and smug and expresses so many things in decimals. I like this coffee about six point two, he says. So smug. But still, he lives in the city. And your lost love lives in the city, whom you still love from afar with a chaste benevolence, and your sister lives in the city, mother of your know-it-all nephew who you like about four point four, and your major love interest lives in the city, and she is interesting. She's been there for you so many times, and there and there. You want to be there for her. She teaches children every day at a school in the city, dozens of children who are ardent about their studies and singing in music class and astronomy with Mr. Myers and soccer when they play the intramural tournament on the grassy field, the Gray versus the Red and the Green versus the Orange because Mr. Demaray in his checkered sweater will let the games go until almost dark, and it all feels like part of a complicated legend. Some nights in the fall, the children run and call and kick the ball until the final whistle blows and they walk back to the yellow windows of the school, their breath plumes in the chilly October air.

•

RON CARLSON is the author of two volumes of poetry and ten books of fiction, most recently *The Blue Box*. He has been heavily anthologized in collections such as *The O. Henry Prize Stories*, *Best American Short Stories*, the *Pushcart Prize* anthology, and *The Norton Anthology of Short Fiction*. He has received numerous awards for his work, including a National Endowment for the Arts Fellowship and a National Society of Arts and Letters Award.

SHAPING AIR

Danielle McLaughlin

From *The Stinging Fly*, Summer 2014

Marco's hands are slender, quick and brutal. They are the hands of a man who shapes air. Together we unload the van, stake out our patch on the scorched summer grass of the fairground. Mothers and children crowd round.

"He'd like a giraffe," says a tall, red-haired woman, pushing forward a boy of about five.

I choose a long, orange balloon and pass it to Marco. He stretches it between his fingers, softening it, then eases it onto the nozzle of the air pump. The mothers shuffle closer. Marco pumps slowly at first, then a little faster, until the balloon begins to swell.

The balloon grows bigger and the mothers grow smaller. They are no longer women but gauche girls, shy and blushing, as if Marco had placed his mouth over theirs and sucked. He slips the balloon off the nozzle, ties it, and the women touch their throats, tug at the necklines of their dresses. I pass him another balloon, watch the way his foot moves up and down on the pump pedal.

Marco runs his hands over the balloons; he presses, twists, and limbs take shape. Another twist: now there is a head, a neck, and—a quick flip onto its stomach—a tail. The balloons make small, high-pitched sounds beneath his fingers. The red-haired woman mutters about the heat, looks to the sky for deliverance.

Before Marco, I knew only the muted balloons of childhood parties, soon discarded and left to wither beneath chairs. That night last summer in the Parco Savello, having watched for hours the weave of his hands, I lay down for him on the parched ground behind the marquee. The stubble of the field was rough against my skin, I heard the thud and spark of bumper cars. He moved slowly, slowly, then faster, and I felt myself expand, every stalk of dry grass needle-sharp and I feared I might burst, and still he pumped, a little more a little more, and still I swelled, my body arcing away from the earth, rising untethered, too much too much, and his mouth was on my breast and he sucked and I shattered, broke in tiny pieces all over the crushed grass.

Marco finishes the giraffe and hands it to the woman. She cradles it, resting her chin on its orange head. I hold out my hand and she stares blankly, before rummaging in her purse for coins. As she walks away, the midday sun illuminates her in silhouette and her red hair blazes. I see Marco's hands, though empty, begin to move. They twist and dart and turn, and as the woman halts and looks back over her shoulder, I feel the air around us change.

•

DANIELLE MCLAUGHLIN's stories have appeared in newspapers and magazines such as the *Irish Times, The South Circular, Southword, The Penny Dreadful, Long Story, Short,* and *The New Yorker.* Her debut collection of short stories, *Dinosaurs on Other Planets,* was published in Ireland in September 2015 by The Stinging Fly Press, and will be published in the UK (John Murray), U.S. (Random House), and Germany (Luchterhand) in 2016.

BAD BOYS

Zack Bean

From *Vestal Review*, Issue 45, Winter 2014

And then the day they tell us that bad boys sometimes leave pennies and nickels on the train tracks to flatten them out, that we should never, never, ever leave coins on the rails, that something as small as a penny could derail a train, send it screeching off the tracks and into the river or the woods; well, of course we run home and lay all our money out onto the rail, little pieces of copper and nickel glistening on that iron bar that stretches off into the afternoon like a perfect dream. Waiting, waiting, one ear to the track, a small vibration, then the approaching rumble and clack and then the conductor waving his arm as the train roars by, the great snake of industry slithering off to wherever, scattering flattened little discs of metal in its wake. We look for them in the gravel, and whose was whose doesn't seem to matter anymore, because none of it will spend—the money has been devalued, pressed into shapes the man at the corner store won't recognize.

One of us shows our father, and he shakes his head in disbelief. *A quarter? You wasted a whole quarter?*

But we like them more now, the way they've been smoothed out and disfigured by metal on metal, the way no two look the same. Yes, we understand why bad boys do this. Train versus pennies, we understand. We could spend a fortune like this.

And nobody has to tell us what else the bad boys do—we've already slipped into the natural order of things. Like predators who've picked up a fresh scent, we're sniffing out our paths, through fistfights and broken windows, through cigarettes and jewelry that nobody paid for, through the bottoms of whiskey bottles and into backseats of old sedans with girls whose names we've forgotten, and on and on through the endless nights—through hawkbill knives and tire irons and Saturday night specials, through twenty-nine days in jail in Little Rock, Arkansas, through the trains we jumped and the jobs we couldn't keep and the silver handcuffs that made perfect circles around our wrists again and again, perfect circles, and through the river of our mothers' tears that we swam across to get to this place where we sit, writing letters to sons we've never met, saying, *Listen, save your pennies, save your nickels, stay away from trains,* even though we know it's already too late.

•

ZACK BEAN's stories have appeared in *Fiction*, *Memorious*, *Cream City Review*, and other literary magazines. His collection of short stories, *Man on Fire*, is forthcoming from ELJ Publications in February 2016. He teaches creative writing and literature at Montana State University.

NIGHTS IN PARADISE

Rusty Barnes

From *Revolution John*, November 2014

Before Paradise

Like Krakatoa—Kilauea—Vesuvius –Mr. McGurk said as he turned to Helen, his lips like red rash. He dropped to his knees. Every rumble of my intestines is for you. Please say that you will have me and we will make calderas together under the stony light. Helen paused, her blaze-orange vest flapping in the breeze as she directed traffic into and out of the Topsfield Fair parking lot. Sorry, she coughed. I just don't burn for you like that.

The Last Night in Paradise

Mrs. McGurk found the newspaper floating in the forsythia, late again. That little shit of a delivery boy. She'd get him this time. She loaded her shotgun with her dearest unspoken wishes, made a plate of lemon cookies for afterward and waited. About four a.m. he showed up and she shot at him, but missed. He lay on her front porch like an asthmatic baby, mouth opening and closing. That's right, she said. Suffer. The news is important.

On Another Night in Paradise

Helen McGurk rose and prepared a lovely rare roast beef for her husband's dinner. She rubbed in salt and pepper with her bare hands, shelled peas, and boiled some potatoes into paste. Mr. McGurk came through the door around five, said hi honey in his sweet voice, only to find her on the table, legs spread, roast toppled, peas scattered, potatoes in her hair. Drive me like a stolen car, baby, she said.

He appreciated her sudden candor.

•

RUSTY BARNES, a member of the National Book Critics Circle, has published three books of poems and three books of fiction, including the flash fiction collection *Breaking it Down* and the novel *Reckoning*. His work has appeared in over two hundred journals and anthologies, among them *Post Road*, *Change Seven*, *Red Rock Review*, *Barn Owl Review*, and *Interstice*. He edits the acclaimed literary journal *Night Train*, and is sole proprietor of *Fried Chicken and Coffee*, a blogazine of rural and Appalachian literature and concerns.

THIS KIND OF LIFE KEEPS BREAKING

Maureen Seaton

From *Narrative*, Fall 2014

AN iSTORY

Times you turn into an eagle counter or an urban park ranger. You're on your own, a fox, a gypsy moth. Near Cañon City, Colorado, the highest bridge in the U.S. spans Royal Gorge, acts as a magnet for melancholy—a tourist might actually see someone jump. Search and rescue is harder to find. Local firefighters are exhausted. "We're not like other species," you say, a river guide, a novelist at night. Your fellow rafters nod, though no one knows for sure what you mean. "Be on the lookout," you add, with a dip of your paddle. Swallows miss you by inches, iridescent and soaring. The river's a prism of three million years, the silence after rapids tremulous. Rocks rise a thousand feet into unforgiving air. This kind of life keeps breaking your heart.

•

MAUREEN SEATON has authored a memoir, *Sex Talks to Girls*, and sixteen poetry collections. Her awards include the Iowa Poetry Prize, Lambda Literary Award, a National Endowment for the Arts Fellowship, and her work has been honored in both the *Pushcart Prize* anthology and *Best American Poetry*. She is Professor of Creative Writing at the University of Miami, Florida.

OBJECT

Naomi Telushkin

From *Bartleby Snopes*, July 2014

The mother told me I could nap in the guest room. She showed me a bedroom with white sheets and a white blanket, no hint of anyone there. But the closet was full of clothing. A prom dress, taffeta, ripped jeans. A lavender bikini. I found out later that her girl became a man, that her daughter took hormones, grew a beard, and brought home a girlfriend. I found out later that the daughter's voice changed and her muscles changed, but her hands stayed small. I found out that they weren't speaking, mother and son, because the mother viewed this new man as a kidnapper. He had kidnapped her beautiful daughter, burned off her hair, ripped off her breasts.

I met the man and fell in love with him. I wasn't expecting to. A man that new. He was rough and delicate, like espresso. I fell in love but it was casual for him, just some wine, a few fleeting nights.

We did not talk about parents; we never got that intimate. I did not tell him I walked his mother's dog, watered her orchards. I did not tell him that I'd tried the bikini on after I knew it was his, that I'd slipped on the lavender string bikini, size eight, that it fit me perfectly—well, only a little loose on top. I did not tell him the strings behind my neck and at my hips felt like hands, like his hands, that I tried different poses, my arms stretched out above my head, my hips thrust out, that I wore it underneath a pencil skirt and buttoned up blouse for a job interview and the office secretary said I was "radiant."

•

NAOMI TELUSHKIN taught creative writing at the University of Singapore. The recipient of the Charles Jonson Award in Fiction from *Crab Orchard Review*, her work has also been published in *Prairie Schooner, Word Riot*, and *The Potomac*, among others. She is completing her MFA in Fiction from Arizona State University and is the host of the podcast "Unpublished Fiction" with Spaghetti on the Wall Productions, set to launch in 2015.

DEAD GARY

Dan Moreau

From *Workers Write! More Tales from the Cubicle*
(Blue Cubicle Press, 2014)

At nine Gary trudged into his cubicle with his sack lunch. He looked awful. He never looked good to begin with but now he looked really bad. It wasn't our place to tell him. He'd find out on his own, we figured. Except he kept showing up each morning. Same clip-on tie, same polyester pants, same short-sleeve front pocket shirt, same brown orthopedic shoes. He was dead all right, paler than usual. He smelled like the dead, so much so that his cubemates hung scented pine trees on their computers. But his numbers were great. You couldn't argue with that. No bathroom breaks, no lunch breaks, no water-cooler talk. All he did was work. No one had the heart to break the news, not even HR, which had taken him off the books. His benefits had been cut, too. The IT guys hadn't gotten around to deactivating his login and probably wouldn't get around to it for six months.

No one knew Gary very well. He liked Mountain Dew and M&Ms and Subway. From what we later pieced together he had died on his living room sofa watching a repeat of *Seinfeld*. Days went by without anyone bothering to check in on him. Tired of waiting around for a funeral and a burial, he did what any one of us would do in his situation; he went to work.

At his quarterly performance evaluation, his supervisor, Bob, smoothed his tie while he looked at Gary's numbers. "Everything looks great here, Gary. Whatever you're doing, keep it up," Bob said. Bob actually didn't know Gary was dead, which didn't surprise us. He was the last one in our office to know anything.

On Dead Gary's birthday, everyone played it cool. We got him a cake, sang happy birthday in the break room, overdosed on sugar. Gary seemed genuinely happy and touched. No one ate the cake, though. As he leaned in to blow out the candles, flecks of his rotting skin peppered the frosting. His skin was looking downright greenish. His nose hung off his face by a shred of skin so that it flapped back and forth while he breathed.

To offset the smell in the office, we conspired with the building engineer to lower the temperature to meat locker temperatures. We wore puffy jackets while we worked. We didn't mind it. It was better than the smell and it seemed to halt Gary's decaying process.

After a while, we quit caring. There was little difference between Dead Gary and Alive Gary. We stopped worrying about telling him the truth. What was the harm in letting him believe he was still alive? Not to say there weren't problems. When his nose finally fell off he stapled it back to his face. Same with his pinkie finger.

December rolled around. With the cooler temps, we gave the air conditioner a break. When we drew names for Secret Santa, I had the bad luck of getting Gary. What do you give a dead guy? Embalming fluid? Foundation makeup? Instead I got him a book of Dilbert cartoons. Gary loved them and every few minutes we could hear him laughing from his cubicle. He posted a few cartoons on his cube walls.

At the Christmas party, Gary had a blast. He danced with everyone, sang, and wore a red Santa's hat. We had never seen Gary so happy. He tried kissing me under the mistletoe, but I wagged my finger at him, saying maybe next year. I don't think anyone had the heart or the stomach to kiss Gary.

The pink slips arrived in January. Corporate wanted to wait till after the New Year to break the news. During my last week, I printed as many résumés, pilfered as much stationery, and applied to as many jobs as I could. Some people took the news in stride; they'd collect unemployment for a year and then start looking for a job in earnest, by which time hopefully the economy would have improved. Some thought about grad school. I just wanted a job. And there was Gary. Because he was no longer on payroll, he didn't actually receive a pink slip.

On the last day, people hugged and carried their potted plants, framed pictures and children's drawings to their car. Emails were exchanged. Promises were made to stay in touch. By three, everyone was gone except me and Gary, who was still working. I leaned over his cubicle and said, "It's over, Gary. You can go home."

He was almost done, he said. He just needed another few minutes to finish up. I carried my box of belongings down the hall and turned off the lights.

•

DAN MOREAU has published fiction in *The Carolina Quarterly*, *Chicago Quarterly Review*, *Gargoyle,* and *The Journal*. He is the recipient of a grant from the Elizabeth George Foundation and was the 2013 English language winner of the *Museum of the Word* Flash Fiction contest.

THE GARDEN SKY

Dave Petraglia

From *Necessary Fiction*, November 26, 2014

Most of all Krista wanted Thuy Luu's eyes. There wasn't much about the young civil engineer that the American didn't like. Now, the quiet dry restaurant after several sprints in and among downpours at the Tan Son Nhat terminal and the rice wine conspired to sink Krista into a warm and willing place, luxuriating in a fuzzy, jet-lagged convalescence.

She'd just explained to Thuy that the app included a silhouetting feature, which used the phone's camera to identify munitions by their shape. Thuy said, those warm, exquisite dark eyes widening as if what she was about to share was as much a revelation to her: "You know in this country we have dirt as clinging as the *gạo nếp.*" She tumbled a lump of sticky rice with her chopsticks. She added, "Most ordnance is caked with soil and unrecognizable when *unearth,*" that last word not in the past tense which Krista was sure she knew well enough, having mastered English as a child. She said it this way with the chopsticks hovering over her bowl as she stared absentmindedly at them, to emphasize the difference between their worlds. This, to Krista, was just as uncalled for as was bringing up the issue of the silhouette problem. They'd exchanged enough application briefs over the last year to understand that the feature was meant to be used to identify *"market bombs,"* those cleaned and presented for sale in public places.

No matter, Krista added, as the app now had an interface to the next generation of detectors to allow identification of the ordnance size type and orientation by magnetic signature.

Krista was not surprised why was she so attracted to Thuy, an appeal having started months before, uninvited, during those scratchy Skypes at odd hours. And memorably, during Thuy's long-distance participation in a meeting in Dallas when, at the moment the grainy image of shabbily home-made prosthetic legs was flashed onto the conference room whiteboard, a sniggered *"chopsticks"* abused the quiet. Krista, pained as others were at that moment, wanted to know if Thuy had heard it. She asked if the image had come through, to which Thuy said yes she could see the limbs and that one looked just like the one she and her brother helped make for their father, which he used for years and kept as a reminder *still.* Her voice was louder than it had been, no doubt she'd adjusted her input such, and she said *"still"* as *"ste-uw,"* the Central Highlands dark *l* emphasized comically, aimed at someone in that darkened room half a world away.

The lights came up that moment under her hand and Krista announced a short break. In the restroom, she thought of Thuy's parents biding the doom from thudding skies; how the smoke clearing the smaller craters revealed shapes bulbous and gray-dull and others long and shiny, from walled thickets of splintered bamboo or oozing paddy banks their dull stenciled hieroglyphs and white chalked English epithets and cartooned genitalia fading with the squeals and curiosity of their youth, then folding into the sticky earth, forgotten. From which the bombs should shed their soil crusts and wriggle free, return to the sky to fix themselves to the wings of remembered planes filling the sunset, and restore to Thuy and her father and brother, all.

•

DAVE PETRAGLIA is a writer and photographer who lives in Florida. His work has appeared in many journals including *Agave, Apeiron, Arcadia, Cactus Heart, Chicago Literati, Crack the Spine, Dark Matter, eFiction India, Far Enough East, Loco, Necessary Fiction, NewPopLit, Prick of the Spindle, Stoneboat, theNewerYork, Up the Staircase,* and *Vine Leaves.* He blogs at DrowningBook.

BEFORE THE SHOT

Valerie Vogrin

From *Bartleby Snopes*, November 2014

—Sing Sing, 1928

I didn't want him to take the assignment. His bosses are
using him and he knows it. He's the bland Midwesterner
who won't be recognized by the local cops and prison brass.
My husband is not one to violate the rules, but he has a
certain hunger to make a bigger name for himself. And I'm
guessing he hopes that a good clear picture of a woman
in Old Sparky will be disturbing enough to change some
people's minds. The night before he left for New York he
nursed a glass of Rhine wine as he sat on a neat rectan-
gle of newspaper wearing just his union suit polishing his
shoes. He swiped polish on his cordovan wingtips with neat
daubs. The rest of him is put together like a longshoreman,
but Will's wrists are on the dainty side. His watch strap
had slipped around so the face rested against his pulse.
He wouldn't let me help him pack. "I don't want you to
have any part of this," he said. He picked out his freshest
shirts, the least worn pairs of black hose. He won't strap the
camera onto his ankle until he is ready to enter the prison
building.

I didn't want him to do it. God knows he's taken some
grisly shots, lots of young—middle-aged—old tough guys
limp-crumpled-knocked off their feet, the camera's bulb

illuminating their comb-furrowed, brilliantined hair although their necks/trunks/abdomens have been pierced by gunfire. Mobsters, thugs, pros, bystanders. Bodies in alleys, gullies, underpasses, basements, and automobile trunks. Last year there was a family. At first, it looked as though the inhabitants of the house simply had been overtaken by fatigue. A young mother slumped in an easy chair, legs straight out, feet slightly splayed. A baby crawling, rump-up, halfway across a dark rug. A man sitting with his young daughter on their sofa listening to the radio, his arm slung tenderly over her shoulder. A second glance and then you saw the small caliber bullet holes where their left eyes should have been. That one took something out of him. The next morning I watched him willing himself to swallow each bite of breakfast and keep it down.

This job's a twist since more than nine times out of ten it's the victims he shoots. The corpses suggest a sequence of events but they cannot confirm or deny. They are buried with their secrets. Today's subject is alive, the infamous adulteress, an American murderess, a woman last photographed in a jaunty feather-topped hat and fur coat and smirk (but I don't guess she's worn those in some time). What I'm afraid of is that he'll see her before they fasten the straps of the leather mask over her face. Although they might blindfold her before they bring her in, my bet is that the powers that be will want her to get a good long look at the chair before she's seated in it. I didn't want him to do it because he wanted to join his father in the florist shop but the old man refused, said no son of his was going to take the kind of guff he'd endured for a career spent in flowers, but his father doesn't have one kind bone in his body and that's why he never had a day's peace among the enamored and grieving. How Will got from bouquets and funeral wreaths to crime photographer I do not know.

Most nights he grinds his teeth, ruining his molars. He's told me more than once that I look like an angel while I sleep. I don't remind him that all of the actual angels were male. I've always looked young for my age. I was 25 when we met, but he believed me when I said I was 18. That I was an orphan. That I'd lost my job as a seamstress because of my eye condition. I know I'm not being clear. And I'm not saying my crimes are anything like hers. What I'm saying is that I am certain that given the opportunity he will look her straight in the face, believing it's the honorable thing to do, seeing as how he will be taking something from her—1/50th of one of her last living seconds. And say he fastens his gaze on her features. Say something in the firm set of her lips or the steel in her pale eyes reminds him of me. What happens after that, I wonder. When he comes home and sees me for what I am.

•

VALERIE VOGRIN is the author of the novel *Shebang*. Her short stories have appeared in print journals such as *Ploughshares*, *AGNI*, and *The Los Angeles Review*, as well as online at *Wigleaf* and *Prick of the Spindle*. In 2010 she was awarded a Pushcart Prize. She is prose editor of *Sou'wester* and teaches at Southern Illinois University–Edwardsville.

THE CANYON WHERE THE COYOTES LIVE

Bobbie Ann Mason

From *New World Writing*, Spring 2014

She lives near a canyon with four cats. The Post-it notes on the bulletin board keep track of the cats—their special needs, the diets, the vet appointments, little notes about their charming pranks and romps.

Yesterday she recorded Annie chirping at a snail. Normally Annie chirps at the sparrows who bathe in a bowl outside the large window.

Billy chirped at an invisible fly. He was leaping high into the air, reaching and chattering. Carrie and Davy have other hobbies—spiders and tiny furry fake mice, respectively.

The cats do not go outside because of the canyon where the coyotes live.

There is a husband around the house, too.

"That sounds like a children's book," he says. "*The Canyon Where the Coyotes Live*, something written to scare children."

"But stories like that make them laugh," she says.

If there were children, she thinks.

She would love to see the cats play outside, but the coyotes from the canyon come forth at night. Even in the daytime coyotes have been sighted. It would be delightful to see the cats on the patio stalking the sparrows, where the coyotes come to stalk the cats. It would be even more delightful to see a toddler pulling a cat's tail.

"Everything's gotta eat," he says, closing the refrigerator door. "Including me," he says.

"Have a Pop-Tart," she says.

"Pop-Tarts are for kids. Why do we have Pop-Tarts?"

Exactly.

He works late shifts in the bottling industry. Often when he comes in late in the night he tells of a coyote crossing the road or an animal he can't identify that always must be a bear or a cougar.

In the night while he is gone the sounds are magnified, and the howling coyotes seem to be at the back door but may be across the canyon. She hears the cat at the scratching post, the *click click click* of the door lock when he returns—if it is him and not some mugger who has commandeered his car and made him drive home at gunpoint.

Yesterday he said to her, "Don't you see how nuts you're becoming? Everything is fraught with terror and apocalypse with you!"

"Fraught? I'm fraught with nothing." Empty. Flat-bellied.

"You're afraid to let the cats outside because of the coyotes. If there weren't any coyotes you'd find something else to be afraid of."

"They would get killed on the road."

"Right. See what I mean?"

"It's better for cats to stay indoors. They live longer."

The Pop-Tart is like limp pasteboard. He eyes it ruefully, then her.

"Furthermore," he says, "we are lucky we don't have any kids. I see how you would be with them."

She snatches the Pop-Tart from his hand. "I'll make lunch," she says.

She makes a salad with artichoke hearts and palm hearts. Her own heart could be the centerpiece, ripped out and posed on a platter like the head of John the Baptist. There is nothing to do but dance.

•

BOBBIE ANN MASON is an American novelist, short story writer, essayist, and literary critic from Kentucky. Her widely anthologized short story "Shiloh" and her novel *In Country* are often taught in classes, and her latest novel is *The Girl in the Blue Beret*. Her work frequently appeared in *The New Yorker* and received many prestigious awards, including the PEN/Hemingway Award, the PEN/Faulkner Award, the National Book Critics Circle Award, and an Arts and Letters Award for Literature from the American Academy of Arts and Letters.

CORRESPONDENCE

Claire Joanne Huxham

From *Neon Literary Magazine*, Issue 38, July 2014

We shared the same birthday, you and I. It seemed like it was fate. I saw you that first time in the newspaper; one of the older girls had left it stuffed down the side of the sofa and I was flicking through it, waiting for the next lesson. Sat around the common room arguing over which tape to stick on. Smell of cheap body spray and sweat. I wore my hair centre-parted and refused to have it cut, not even trimmed. You looked at me—a matrix of dots printed into a pattern. Your eyes were so black. It's funny how it can all start like that sometimes. I ripped your picture out and shoved it into my bag, flattened in between the pages of *Tricolore*.

Janice thought it was weird when I stuck you up in front of my desk in my bedroom.

"Don't you think it's a bit freaky?" she said. "I mean, you've got him right by Glenn Medeiros and Corey." She meant Haim. They were on first name terms now.

I shrugged. "It's just a picture."

1988: nearly the end of a decade. We wore Bermuda shorts and decorated our roller skates with Day-Glo laces. I came to an agreement with Mum that I'd get my hair cut if I could have a perm. It stuck out in a magnificent triangle from my neck. The '90s loomed: unknowable, unformulated, nebulous. We were poised, on the cusp. We wanted it and we didn't. But we knew we couldn't turn back.

I would have put your photo up on the mantelpiece if I'd been allowed, with all the family portraits and pictures of rabbits and cats. Instead I stuck you up on the inside door of my wardrobe. I thought about writing to you but I wasn't sure what to say. Janice and I sat on the bobbly rug Mum had brought back from Tenerife and plotted our futures with pink pens on large sheets of paper. We drew houses and cars and money and clothes. We wrote a list of potential husbands and back-ups if Donnie Wahlberg wasn't interested (Janice was fickle in her affections). We had it all mapped out.

Life without the possibility of parole. That's how long they gave you. In a way it was reassuring, knowing that wherever I went, no matter how far, you'd always be in the same place, charting your time by the angle of the sun and the turn of the seasons. You were there when I left school and we all signed each other's shirts with fat marker pens, writing good luck. And again when I dropped out of university after six months. You stood in the shadows. When the photo turned yellow and brittle I took it down and kept it in a box full of old cards and gig tickets. I felt relieved somehow. Instead I run this letter to you, that I'll never send, over in my head. Trying to work out exactly what I mean to say.

One day soon we'll meet under a harsh Texan sun. The dust rises in a gritty haze, in whirlpools and sudden drifts. A warm wind blows. Some say coyotes roam here and steal babies, pulling them into the night. They gather in circles and drink their blood. We'll sit on wooden benches bleached almost white in the penitentiary yard. Your face so lined, your feet and hands shackled. And you'll say, "What took you so long?"

•

CLAIRE JOANNE HUXHAM is based in the UK and has been writing flash fiction and poetry since 2010. Her work appears in various places online and in print, including *Necessary Fiction*, *Metazen*, *Monkeybicycle*, and *Foundling Review*. She is currently working on a dystopian road trip novel.

BEST SMALL FICTIONS 2015
FINALISTS

AIDAN ROONEY
Habitation (*The Stinging Fly*)

AJAY VISHWANATHAN
Blanks (from *From a Tilted Pail*, Queen's Ferry Press)

AKI SCHILZ
Heat Wave (*Cheap Pop*)

ALAN ELYSHEVITZ
Deep (*Mid-American Review*)

ALLISON ADAIR
Letter to My Niece, in Silverton, Colorado (*Mid-American Review*)

ANDREW RIDKER
From the Diary of Your Unlived Life (*SmokeLong Quarterly*)

ARLENE ANG
Rupture (from *Banned for Life*, Misty Publications)

BRIAN DOYLE
The Stigmata (*The MOON*)

BRUCE HOLLAND ROGERS
Advice and Consent (*KYSO Flash*)

CALVIN Z. HEYWARD
Carolina blooms (*Haibun Today*)

CHERISE WOLAS
Another Way to Use a Train Station (*Blue Fifth Review: Blue Five Notebook Series*)

CHRIS L. TERRY
Real Skater Music (*Hobart*)

CHRISTINA SANDERS
Grass (*Litro*)

CHRISTOPHER MERKNER
Permission (*DIAGRAM*)

CLAUDIA SMITH
Big Sky (*Corium*)

CURTIS SMITH
Bluecurls and Aster (*Blue Fifth Review: Blue Five Notebook Series*)

Dena Afrasiabi
Home (*JMWW*)

Elizabeth Brown
A Good Night for Maali (*Hermeneutic Chaos Literary Journal*)

Eric Shonkwiler
Nettle Creek Cemetery (*Cheap Pop*)

Grant Miller
We Should Have Named Him (*Qu Literary Journal*)

Hun Ohm
Photographic Memory #5 (*Literary Orphans*)

Ioanna Mavrou
My Copy (*Litro*)

Jesi Bender
Linda (*Split Lip Magazine*)

Jesse Kohn
Doing It (*SAND*)

Joanna Penn Cooper
Dates with Artists (from *The Itinerant Girl's Guide to Self-Hypnosis*, Brooklyn Arts)

Kara Vernor
Crash (*Atticus Review*)

Katey Schultz
The Last Thing They Might Have Seen (*KYSO Flash*)

Kathy Fish
Strings (*New World Writing*)

Kiik A. K.
An Egg (*matchbook* lit mag)

Lauren Becker
Every Day Is Christmas (from *If I Would Leave Myself Behind*, Curbside Splendor)

Leesa Cross-Smith
Bearish (*NANO Fiction*)

Lindsay Fisher
Cordelia Holds Eddie's Heart in Her Hands (*1000words*)

Malachi McIntosh
Paint by Numbers (*Flash: The International Short-Short Story Magazine*)

Marc Cinanni
Ping (*Matchbook Stories*)

Mathew Sharpe
Two (from "Three Very Short Stories," *Monkey Business International*)

Mathew Vasiliauskas
Bancroft Street (*SAND*)

Max Vande Vaarst
Wovoka (*JMWW*)

Meg Pokrass
Ringing (*Green Mountains Review*)

Nin Andrews
The Price of Red Buckle Shoes (*KYSO Flash*)

OWEN VINCE
"to my brother in the water"
(*1000words*)

PETER BUTLER
Things in My Attic (*Haibun Today*)

RYAN WERNER
If There's Any Truth in a North-bound Train (*SmokeLong Quarterly*)

SALADIN AHMED
592 (*Nanoism*)

SAM MARTONE
Ferry Tale (*Wigleaf*)

SAM WILSON
Five Wigs (*Vestal Review*)

SCHULER BENSON
Stroke Test (from *The Poor Man's Guide to an Affordable, Painless Suicide*, Alternating Currents)

SHELDON LEE COMPTON
Fall Gently in the Gray Woods of Our Death (*New World Writing*)

STEVE KARAS
Catching Fire (*WhiskeyPaper*)

TARA LASKOWSKI
Vanna (*Atticus Review*)

TRACEY UPCHURCH
Vinegar (from *Eating My Words: 2014 National Flash-Fiction Day Anthology*, Gumbo)

SPOTLIGHT ON *PLEIADES:*
LITERATURE IN CONTEXT

Best Small Fictions: Give us a brief summation of the history of *Pleiades*.

Phong Nguyen, Ed.: *Pleiades* began in 1980 as a photocopied, staple-bound student literary journal under the advisement of UCM faculty member Bob Jones. Jones was, among other things, a mentor to David Baker, who is currently poetry editor for *Kenyon Review*. In the early 1990s, Rose Marie Kinder expanded the mission of the journal to include a diverse roster of new writers from throughout the country. When Kevin Prufer joined the magazine in 1998, he raised the profile of the journal to include nationally known writers such as Joyce Carol Oates, Sherman Alexie, and D. A. Powell. Together with Wayne Miller, who joined the journal as coeditor in 2006, Prufer brought *Pleiades* to an international audience and filled the journal with international content, emphasizing works in translation from around the world. I joined the journal as fiction editor in 2007, becoming coeditor with Wayne Miller in 2010. I'm now sole editor. My contributions so far have been to increase the web presence of the journal and draw attention to the quality of our prose offerings.

BSF: Congratulations on getting 3 out of 3 nominations on to the finalist list, and then accepted into the book ("Scale,"

Michael Martone; "A Notice from the Office of Reclamation," J. Duncan Wiley; "Wimbledon," Seth Brady Tucker). They are all so different. In your editor's opinion, what unites them as successful flashes?

PN: Successful flash fictions share one quality, in my view. They all suggest a much larger context—a story that is far vaster than the words on the page. All good stories perform this same transformation, but when it comes to flash fiction, that quality really comes into focus. It's Hemingway's iceberg analogy amplified tenfold. I'm also interested in the way that flash fiction establishes voice, because most flash fictions are about the length that it takes most long stories to establish voice, so the flash voice has to *become* the story in a huge way. Lastly, all three stories succeed in *different* ways, because in some way all flash fictions are experiments, and the experiment each one undertakes is different, but they all hold in common the ability to commit to the experiment and not be dragged down by the need to hew to traditional ideas of art and craft in making fiction.

BSF: How do small fictions fit into the past, present, and future at your journal?

PN: Flash fiction is something that has been a part of *Pleiades* ever since I became editor. It will always have a place at the magazine. As long as our contributors continue to write these stellar short-short stories, I will continue to publish them. In addition to the three fiction writers appearing in this anthology, I know a number of *Pleiades* poets who have written some extremely successful flash fictions, and I am interested in the borders of flash fiction and prose poetry.

SPOTLIGHT ON MICHAEL MARTONE

Best Small Fictions: Congratulations on having two of your small fictions accepted into the 2015 edition. You are one of the most prolific writers in this genre and seem to have a limitless imagination and a gift for condensed, poetic writing. Where and how do you think this developed?

Michael Martone: Well, you are very kind for saying so. Prolific? It seems I just try to do a little bit every day and over all the days I have been around, these drips and drabs add up. And limitless? I think there is a little paradox there. Limits are important. In geometry, a bounded space contains an infinite number of points. That is to say, you can't have a "limitless" imagination until you imagine the limits. And where do I trace this development? Bloomington, Indiana. As an undergraduate student I was taking a poetry workshop where we would argue about line breaks. I was so frustrated that I went home and typed up my next poem (I used, back then, a typewriter, kids!) breaking the line when the bell dinged. The result was, well, prose. Also in that class, a poet would say it took him 3 or 4 years to write this or that poem. So I tried writing a poem in 3 or 4 minutes. That year too I was a founding member of a group called RKO Radio Poems that wrote poems on demand all over town.

We charged a quarter a poem. Our slogan was: A poem must not mean but be twenty-five cents. With that stunt I came to appreciate quantity of writing more than quality. I just wrote things and did not worry so much about the goodness or badness.

BSF: "Scale" (p. 71) and "WordCross" (p. 74) are linked by the same main character, Art Smith. Is he a real aviator? And are the stories going to be part of a larger work?

MM: Yes, he was an earlier aviation pioneer from my hometown, Fort Wayne, Indiana. Great name, yes? Art Smith. He began flying right after the Wright Brothers. Died in a plane crash in 1926. Once the airplane was invented there was an argument about what should be done with this new technology. One school wanted to create stable and safe platforms for cargo and passengers and the other wanted to see what this new machine could do. Smith was in the latter group. So he was one of the first to do an inside loop-the-loop, a barrel roll, an outside loop. And also, it is said, he invented skywriting. So that means the first writing in the sky took place in the air over my hometown. There is little real documentation of his "writing" however. A mention of writing LUCKY STRIKE over Detroit. A photo of night writing in San Francisco. So my book, the larger work, is called *The Collected Writings of Art Smith, The Bird Boy of Fort Wayne, Edited by Michael Martone.* A "documentary" of this history. The titles of the pieces will be faux photographs of skywriting and the pieces will be the context of the "photographs," the imagined writing.

BSF: You teach small fictions. If you could give one piece of advice to new writers learning to write "small," what would it be?

MM: Keep a commonplace journal. Or keep a file, scrapbook, folder where you collect examples of different kinds of language fields, rhetoric, styles, voices, syntaxes, inflections, etceteras that you find in the variety of things you read every day. The form of the very short story (like the form of the very long story or novel) is a voracious form. It assumes and consumes other modes—letters, recipes, advertisements, reports, speeches, ballyhoos, manuals, whatever. A commonplace book, where you wield the X-ACTO knife more than the pencil or pen, can nudge you out of language and form that is "literary," I think. Also, actual cutting and pasting can make you conscious of the material nature of the art that is often overlooked, attempting to create texts that are "transparent." Feel the artifice-ness of the artifice it creates. And also pay attention to the contexts in which you discover the tidbits of prose and how the same words in the same order transform when you reframe them.

ABOUT THE GUEST EDITOR

ROBERT OLEN BUTLER has published fifteen novels and six volumes of short stories, one of which, *A Good Scent from a Strange Mountain*, won the 1993 Pulitzer Prize for Fiction, and three of which—*Severance, Intercourse*, and *Weegee Stories*—are comprised entirely of small fictions (225 in all). He has also published an influential volume of his lectures on the creative process, *From Where You Dream*. Butler has twice won a National Magazine Award in Fiction, and among his numerous other awards are a Guggenheim Fellowship; the Richard and Hinda Rosenthal Foundation Award from the American Academy of Arts and Letters; and the F. Scott Fitzgerald Award for Outstanding Achievement in American Literature. His stories have appeared in such publications as *The New Yorker, Esquire, Harper's, The Atlantic Monthly, GQ, Zoetrope, The Paris Review, Granta, The Hudson Review, The Virginia Quarterly Review, Ploughshares*, and *The Sewanee Review*. His stories have been chosen for inclusion in four annual editions of *The Best American Short Stories*, eight annual editions of *New Stories from the South*, and two *Pushcart Prize* volumes. His works have been translated into twenty-one languages, including Vietnamese, Thai, Korean, Polish, Japanese, Serbian, Farsi, Czech, Estonian, Greek, and most recently Chinese. He teaches creative writing at Florida State University in Tallahassee, Florida.

CPSIA information can be obtained at www.ICGtesting.com
Printed in the USA
BVOW02s0045270116

434355BV00001B/20/P